The First Cut

Part One of The Barbershop Quartet

A.R. Ryder

ISBN: 978-1-8384993-1-0

The First Cut

On the outside, Mac seems to have it all: he's good looking, confident, happy-go-lucky, solvent, and even has his own business in London.

He also has girlfriends that come and go, lots of them - and that's the problem. He can't find love - or rather he is unwilling to allow himself to fall in love. For Mac, for all his outward charm, is damaged goods. He is a man emotionally scarred by a cut so deep, so severe, that he shields himself from love.

And he's happy with that. Mac's doing just fine.

That is until the day Alice walks into his life…

The Barbershop Quartet

The First Cut
The Next Cut
The Deepest Cut
The Final Cut

ARRyder.com

The
First Cut

ARRyder.com

Chapter 1: Mac

Today's sort of an important day for me. I'm interviewing, as in interviewing someone who wants a job in Mac the Clipper, a barbershop I own and run in this busy part of North London. That bastard Jack, who'd worked for me for a couple of years, jumped ship and went to work for Top Cutz, with a 'z', a barber downtown run by a man I know called Ian. I told Jack he was crazy, that his new boss was a jerk and would work him so hard he'd go home dead on his feet. And for what? The pay was the same, maybe a few pennies in the hour better off, but that's what made the difference apparently. And, I'm telling you, I'm not wrong here – I know Ian of old and he's a nasty piece of work.

So, yeah – Jack. I'd always seen Jack as a decent sort of bloke so I was disappointed by his decision to leave, can't pretend otherwise. As the boss, you try not to take it personally, but it was difficult because that's exactly how it felt – personal. Deeply so. We shook hands as he left. Me and the other boys here wished him luck and all that usual sort of shit. He promised to keep in touch but I thought *why bother, mate?*

Once you leave and walk out that door, things can never be the same. Just go, mate, sling your hook and don't darken this place ever again.

So today, I'm interviewing for Jack's replacement. This is what I'm officially looking for…

1. An experienced barber.
2. Customer experience.
3. Someone good with people.
4. Decent command of English.

And this is what I'm really looking for…

5. A cool barber.
6. Male.
7. Young (but no teenagers).
8. Good looking.
9. Confident.
10. Likes a laugh.
11. Ripped.

And on my 'desirable' list:

12. Got a beard
13. Got tattoos.
14. A few piercings (but not to the point of it looking freaky).
15. Into motorbikes.

So, I'm not asking for much.

OK, I appreciate that a lot of stuff on my lists is subjective, like exactly how many visible piercings does a guy need to have when it stops being cool and steps over the boundary into the freakish zone? Tattoos? I love the tatts. I've got them all up and down both arms, and a semi-circular one across my chest, and one that snakes down from my belly button to my pants. But again, it's about knowing when to stop. So, no face tattoos, thanks very much. And how confident is confident, how handsome is good looking? After all, our clientele is one hundred percent male (excluding the mums that bring in their kids). So, we don't need to be particularly *attractive*, frankly, we could all look like Quasimodo and get away with it, so why does it matter? Because somehow… it *does*.

Things I'm not bothered about:

1. Sexuality (a hole's a hole as far as I'm concerned).
2. Marital status (as it is, we're all single, not one girlfriend between us).
3. Race (the guy can be green, as long as he can cut hair and adheres to the above list).

Problem is, I've only got two interviewees and, this is the weird thing, one of them is *female*. Yep, some girl wants to work in a barbershop. Nothing wrong with that per se, I'm all for equality, but a woman is going to upset the dynamic here. There's me and my three boys, well, two since Jack buggered off. And frankly, we're all cut from the same mould – late twenties, beards, tattoos, cool haircuts and… male, very, very male. Mac the Clipper positively reeks of testosterone. A female will throw us out of our stride. Will she be interested in motorbikes? Maybe. One shouldn't assume. Will she have tattoos? Hopefully and quite possibly. Will she have a beard?

Well, if she does, she's definitely not working here! I'm looking at her CV. Her name is Alice Sinclair and, to be fair, she's got the experience, she's been cutting hair for years, but, and here's the thing, it's always been with ladies' hairdressers. She's never worked with blokes, and that's an issue. She even mentions it, says she wants to expand her experience. She's due in five minutes. Then, after Alice, I'm interviewing a lad called Calvin.

It's Monday morning so the shop is quiet, just me and Tony. He's busy with a customer, a bloke in his thirties, already losing his hair, poor man, and they're talking shit about the Austrian Grand Prix that was on tele yesterday. I missed it, myself. Had to go see my father. Eoin, my other lad, is due in at lunchtime.

The door swings open, and I leap to my feet, expecting Alice. But it's only the postman. Why am I so jittery?

I pace up and down the shop, turning the music up a notch. Eminem always helps me relax. Not this time though.

'Stop worrying, Mac,' says Tony. 'It'll be fine.'

'Yeah, I know.' I pour myself another coffee. I take a gulp then regret it – I can't be greeting her with coffee breath. So I spray a squirt of breath freshener down my throat. Fact is, it's time. She should be here by now.

Together, the four of us, me, Jack, Tony and Eoin, we were a team, barbers second but friends first and foremost; we were like the Four Musketeers. That's why I'm so pissed off with Jack leaving us like he did, breaking us up. Now, it's just the three of us. We need a fourth member to be whole again, so I'm hoping this Calvin guy fits the bill. He'd better because we can't truly be the Four Musketeers if one of us is a woman. Apparently, 'Eoin' is Irish for Owen. Tony and I are local boys, north London born, north London bred.

Right now I'm too heated up about this woman. Where is she, for fuck's sake? I look at the big clock we have hanging up. She's now officially late. I don't do late; I don't like late. It's disrespectful. It's rude.

'Have you got her number?' asks Tony, as his customer leaves. 'Ring her. Maybe she forgot.'

'Forgot? It's a bloody job interview, why should she forget, for fuck's sake. I'll give her another two minutes.'

I literally count the seconds down on my phone. I feel so wound up now, I actually hope she doesn't turn up. Two minutes pass, three, four, five bloody minutes.

'That's it,' I say. 'I've had enough. If she can't be bothered to get here on time, she can fuck right off…'

Suddenly, I'm vaguely aware of a presence behind me even though I didn't hear the shop door open, didn't see a thing. Tony clears his throat. 'What?' I turn around to where he's looking, and there, standing at the door, is a woman, flustered.

'I'm so sorry I'm late,' she says in a breathless voice. She looks on the verge of tears.

She's a vision with blonde hair that curls beneath her jaw, bright green eyes and a smile to melt a man at twenty paces. She's a good few inches shorter than me, perhaps a whole foot, and she has to look up at me. She steps forward, her hand extended. I take it. It's warm and small within my clasp. She looks down at my hand, perhaps aware of my huge hand gripping hers. I let go, conscious of my size. She's wearing vintage jeans with a studded belt, ankle-high leather boots and a crisp white shirt with large buttons. She takes my breath away. I try not to admire that shirt for too long as she's unaware that she's standing in the light and we can see quite perfectly the shape of her breasts. She smells of sweetness and cinnamon, a giddy combination.

Good God, she's beautiful; my jaw drops as the word 'fuck' quietly slips from my mouth.

Chapter 2: Alice

Did he just say the word 'fuck'?

We shake hands and my knees tremble. This man is all man. I can't remember the last time I've had such a visceral reaction to a man. My god, Alice, get a grip, girl. 'My name is Alice,' I say, aware of the tremor in my voice. 'I've come for the interview.'

'Oh, yes, of course. Yes. Erm… welcome. My name's Thomas, but everyone calls me Mac.'

'How do you do?'

'And this is Tony.'

Tony nods. 'Nice to meet you, love.'

Love? He calls me *love?* How quaint. Still, when you're this good looking, you can call me what you want. Christ on a stick, they're both gorgeous!

'Right,' says Mac, clearing the air. 'If you'd like to follow me.'

Tony steps forward. 'I'll take your coat, if you want.'

I pass him my coat, a rather lovely dark green velvety thing that looks as if it cost a small fortune.

'You've got a great place here,' I say, taking in my surroundings. 'I live nearby and I often pass by, and I've always thought it looks like a great place to work.' It's not true – I never gave the place a second thought until I saw the job advert in the local newspaper. But, to be fair, it would be one mighty cool place to work. The brick walls give off an industrial vibe, and they're covered in framed posters featuring the best – Marlon Brando, Elvis, Bruce Lee in his famous Kung Fu pose, Dolly Parton, guitar in hand, the Fab Four with their cheesy grins.

'Shall we go through?' says Mac. He leads me through to his office at the back, big enough for a desk and a couple of chairs, and a sofa where, I imagine, he kicks off his boots and has a power nap. He invites me in and offers me a coffee. I say yes, white and strong, managing to stop myself just in time from saying *like my men*. Somehow, I feel that might have come across as not entirely appropriate. I don't want to scare the man off. He shouts my coffee order to Tony.

I look at the huge, framed poster of ruggedly handsome Clark Gable and the lovely Vivien Leigh embracing for the film poster of *Gone With the Wind*. 'Don't they look gorgeous?' I say. 'Have you seen it? The film, I mean.'

'It's brilliant. It's perhaps my favourite movie.'

I don't tell him it's perhaps my favourite too – in case it sounds creepy or he thinks I'm just saying it to impress him.

He smiles and looks into my eyes and I feel a little tug of pleasure between my legs. 'Please, take a seat,' he says.

I sit, thanking him.

Now, both seated, he doesn't say anything, he just looks at me until it starts getting just a little awkward. I clear my throat. 'Is there anything you wanted to ask me?' I ask nervously.

'Hm? What? Oh, God, yes. I'm so sorry. You… you remind

me of someone.' Is he lying to me?

Tony re-appears, bearing my coffee. I thank him.

'So,' says Mac, leaning across the desk towards me. 'Tell me about your experience. I read it on your CV but…' He lifts his hands off the desk. 'Remind me.'

I sweep my hair back, exposing my neck. I'm not sure why I did that. I talk and tell him about all the jobs I've had, the experience I've picked up along the way. But is he actually listening? I'm not convinced he is.

'So you worked in your parents' hairdressers?'

I'd already told him but still… 'In the Lake District, yes. A small town called Keswick'

'Keswick? Not heard of it.'

'You should visit one day, it's a beautiful place; you'd like it.'

'I will. Thanks. But you've never worked in a barber's shop, have you? You've never cut men's hair.'

'Only my brother's and my father's.'

'Professionally, I mean.'

Oh dear. I shake my head. 'No. But I imagine it'd be a lot easier than cutting women's hair.'

'Not necessarily,' he snaps, his professional pride slightly hurt.

'I'd love to cut men's hair; I'd love to work here. And the pay's good.'

'We pay the best in London,' he says. 'Do you like football?'

'Football?' I wasn't expecting that! 'It's OK. I can take it or leave.'

'Well, here, you're gonna have to get into football, or soccer as our American customers say. It's literally the number one topic of conversation here, so all of us have had to take an interest and learn about the game. Do you know how the off-side rule works?'

Is he serious? 'No?'

'What famous Frenchman did Arsenal sign last summer?'

'I don't know!'

'Who won the Champions' League last season?'

'Oh, erm… was it Barcelona? No, it was Real Madrid? Erm…' I burst out laughing, I can't help it. 'Manchester United? Chelsea?'

'Keep going and you might get there eventually.'

I shake my head again, still laughing. 'I don't know.'

'Why did you leave your last job?'

I shrug my shoulders and my laughter disappears. 'It just didn't work out.'

'It didn't work out?' he barks. 'You're gonna have to tell me more than that. I'll need a reference, won't I?'

I look down at my lap. 'I can give you all the references you need…'

'Just not the last place you worked?'

'No.'

'Right. OK then.' He leans back in his chair, steepling his fingers. 'So, why do you want to work *here*?'

'I live nearby and I've always thought this looks like a great place to work, it always looks buzzy from outside.'

'But it's all men – male customers, male workers.'

'I love men…' Heck, did I just say that? I turn a bright shade of red. 'What I mean is… I'd like a change. I'd value the challenge.' *Value the challenge*? Christ, where did I pick that up from?

'Tell me why I should take you on?'

I take a sip of my coffee, biding for time. 'Because I'm good with people and I always work with a smile, and I always work hard.' We look at each other. The seconds tick by. I don't like this; I think I've lost him somehow. 'You don't think I'm up to it, do you?'

His answer is immediate. 'I worry because, whatever you reckon, cutting men's hair is a different skill set. It's…'

'Look, it doesn't matter. You're probably right.' I stand. 'It's fine. As it is, I've got another interview this afternoon at the barbers down the road.'

'Top Cutz, spelt with a z? Ian's place?'

'Yeah. I might have more luck there. Thanks anyway.'

'Yeah. Sure.'

I'm at the door. I turn. 'It was nice meeting you.'

'Yeah. And you. Good luck with Ian.'

And then I leave, wondering how and where it all went so wrong.

Chapter 3: Mac

So I put out my ad stating that I had a vacancy two weeks back, and I only got two responses. It didn't surprise me too much, barbers find jobs easily and once they find somewhere, they tend to stick around for years. Alice was one of my two applicants and the other, Calvin, is sitting in the chair in front of me, smothered in his aftershave, looking cocky. My office is smelling strongly of his very sweet and pungent perfume. It catches me in the back of the throat. The way he slouches and crosses his legs, he thinks he's got it all. And he probably has, just not in my shop.

'So then, Calvin, you've got some experience of cutting hair?'

He shrugs his shoulders. 'Yeah, course, mate. Been cutting hair for years, loads of experience.'

'But according to your CV, you're only twenty-one.'

'So what? I've been cutting hair since I was a kid. I know what I'm doing.' He looks up at my poster. 'Gone With the Wind? Is that on Netflix? Looks a bit old, mate.'

'It came out in 1939.'

'Jesus, did they even have Netflix in them days?'

'I don't think so. Anyway, tell me, Calvin, why should I take you on?'

He shrugs his shoulders again, a habit I'm finding rather irritating. 'Because I'm good at what I do.'

'Why did you leave your last job?'

'I got the sack, didn't I?'

'Did you? I don't know. Why did you get the sack?'

'Because the old geezer running the joint took a shine to me, know what I mean? I wasn't having it, and I told him to sod off. So he goes and sacks me, saying I was off sick too much.'

'And were you?'

'What?'

'Off sick too much?'

'Nah, of course not. The bloke was a knob, he was just looking for an excuse because I wouldn't–'

'Yeah, yeah, I get the picture.'

'Are any of the blokes here poofs?'

'You mean gay?'

'Whatever.'

'Well, I don't think…' I stop myself. 'Actually, yes, we all are, Calvin.'

That stops him in his tracks. 'Are you? All of you? Christ.'

'I think we're done here,' I say, picking up a couple of sheets of paper and squaring them up. 'I'll let you see yourself out.'

He can't get out of my office quick enough. The door closes with a bang. 'See you,' I say to the space he's left behind.

Well, that went well.

I open the office window, trying to get rid of Calvin's aftershave. I sit at my desk, my thoughts full of Alice. I wonder if she's being interviewed right this minute by Ian. Surely, she'll see what sort of man he is. Any female under the age of eighty-five and with her own teeth is fair game as far as Ian's concerned. But what choice did I leave her? The way I spoke to her would have put her off for life. I'm my own worst enemy sometimes. If only I could re-live that interview, I'd do it differently, do it *better*. I should know better by now because this isn't the first time I've done this. It's my speciality – sabotaging all interactions with attractive women. Because I know you can't trust women like Alice. They will lure you into their web with their sweet talk and eyelashes, and once you think you've got your life sorted, they'll fuck with you and leave you shattered. OK, I know this is not necessarily true and Alice, I'm sure, is far too nice to be like that but I'm not taking any chances, no way. I've seen it with my own eyes and I'm not risking it; there's too much to lose. I'd rather stay as I am and stay safe, thank you very much.

*

The shop is busy, both Tony and Eoin have got customers, the stereo's on loud, there's a small queue and the place is buzzing. 'OK,' I say loudly. 'Who's next?'

An older guy, one of our regulars, takes his place in my chair. We each have our own barber's chair. Mine is the one furthest from the shop window, next to the sand brick wall, next to Bruce Lee. I wrap the apron around him, sticking the Velcro down at the back of his neck. 'How are you, sir? How's it going? Same cut as always?' The usual patter. Yep, just the same as always. Men are rarely adventurous when it comes to their hair. From Day One, they settle on a style that basically they stick with for years and years, even as they get older and their hair gets thinner and thinner. Always the same. The only time they do risk having something a little different it's because of a woman. Their wife or girlfriend *suggests* they try this or that, the men don't want to, they're happy with the usual, but they always acquiesce in the end, the woman always has her way. It's just life, it's the way it goes. Men – we think we rule the world but of course we all know that ain't true!

Thirty minutes later, I'm finished with my customer. He thanks me, leaves a small tip, and heads out, happy to have crossed this particular chore off his list of things to do today. He'll go home happy, his wife will be pleased and tell him he looks five years younger and all will be well in their world, at least for a short while.

The boys finish with their customers as well. I turn the volume down on the stereo a little and we lounge around on our chairs. Eoin pops a toothpick in his mouth. 'So then, Mac, Tony here was telling me you were entertaining a bit of a babe this morning.'

'No,' says Tony between puffs of his vape. 'Not a bit of a babe but a total, one hundred per cent drop-dead gorgeous babe.'

'Gee,' says Eoin. 'Is this true, Mac?'

'Yeah, well, she was alright–'

'*Alright*?!' screeches Tony.

'Whatever,' I say, unable to keep the irritation out of my voice.

'So, did you give her the job or not?' asks Eoin.

'No. Yes. No. It didn't go too well, if I'm honest.'

'Oh, for fuck's sake, Mac,' says Tony. 'What are you playing at? What do you mean, it didn't go too well? You're not giving it to that arrogant little shit, are you?'

'I might not have any choice.'

'You're bloody not,' says Tony. 'He came in here, sizing everything up and strutting around the place like he owned the joint.'

'Yeah,' says Eoin. 'He spoke to us like we were the best of mates or something. And the way he spoke to the punters, it was like he'd known them for years. I don't want him here.'

'Yeah, but at the end of the day it's my call, isn't it?'

'Right,' says Tony. He takes another puff on his vape and exchanges glances with Eoin. And I know I've upset them both. They're like brothers, those two – one takes umbrage, they both take umbrage. And I've got a rebellion brewing in the ranks, I can feel it.

'Sure,' says Eoin, examining his toothpick. 'Like you say, it's your call, Mac, but I'm telling you now, mate, you hire that little shite and you'll lose Tone and me; we'll be gone before you can shake your metal comb at us.'

I look at Tony. He nods. They're in agreement. 'Phone her,' he says. 'And offer her the job. You'll regret it if you don't, mate.'

I sigh. They're right, of course. They usually are. But I haven't told them she's got an interview at Top Cutz, I can't face telling them. After the way I spoke to her, she'll take Ian's job and not mine, and I'll look like an absolute idiot for having let her slip through my fingers. And, like they said, there's no way I can let Calvin loose on my punters; it'd be a disaster.

A customer comes in, a young lad with a rainbow tee-shirt. He's one of Tony's regulars. They fist bump each other. They know each other well. No one shakes hands in here any more, not since Covid hit. Eoin saunters off to make the lad a cup of coffee. Meanwhile, I've got a phone call to make.

I sit at my desk, feeling rather old all of a sudden. I pick up my phone and swipe in. I check all my social media accounts first, both my ones and the business's, and my email. I watch a few videos on TikTok, trying to wile the time away, putting off what I have to do. I also check in on Facebook and check the account for Sunny Grove Care Home. There's a new post with a few photos attached. I swipe through them quickly, hoping to find my father there and yes, there he is, eating his lunch or rather staring at it with his usual vacant expression. He's wearing collar and tie, as always. He doesn't look particularly happy nor unhappy – just confused. Poor Dad. I'll go see him after work.

Anyway, time is marching on and I can't put it off any longer. Alice would have had her second interview of the day by now. She might be at home or in a café somewhere, deciding who she'd rather have as her future boss – me or Ian. I ring her number. After three rings, an automated voice cuts in: *The number you have called is not available right now.* Really? How odd. I turn off and re-dial, this time paying more attention to the numbers as I punch them in. *The number you have called...* Shit. I check the numbers again, slowly, and yes, I definitely have the right number, the number she put on her CV. Maybe she's still with Ian and she's just turned her phone off. I leave it for five minutes, then try again. And another five minutes, and another...

She's not answering, and I now feel the urgent need to speak to her, to see her even. She put her address on her CV. I look it up on Google Maps, and sure enough, like she said, it's really nearby. She said she passed the shop on a regular basis, so I knew it had to be close. I'd go and see her, knock on her door. *I was just passing so I thought...* I rub my eyes. I'm mad – how could I just turn up at her place? She'd think me weird; she'd call the police, and rightly so.

I go back out to the shop. Eoin is busy, while Tony is talking to a woman and a boy of about nine. The woman and child leave. 'Well?' asks Tony.

'No answer.'

'That's shit then. But you're still not taking on that kid.'

'No, no, that's not gonna happen.'

I pace the shop a while, knowing both of them are looking at me, the sound of the stereo ringing in my ears, the snip, snip, snip of Eoin's scissors hard at work. Why had I treated her so badly? Why did I always go and spoil things? It was like a death wish, a self-destruct button that I just had to press whenever a woman talked to me. It was like I had this inner voice saying, *I like you, I'd like to get to know you better*, while my outer voice is shouting, *Go away, go away*. And of course, Alice only heard the outer voice. *Go away, Alice, go away*. It was time to put an end to this, to stamp on that self-destruct button and destroy it. I refuse to remain a slave to my past a moment longer.

I turn to the boys. 'OK, I'm popping out.'

Eoin stops work for a moment. He and Tony exchange glances.

'I might be a while.' I wink at them. 'Wish me luck.'

*

Alice does indeed not live too far away from the shop, eight minutes or so down a leafy street with attractive Edwardian houses with well-kept manicured front gardens. It's a bright day, the sun shining, the sky a vibrant blue. As I walk down her street, my anxiety goes up a notch with every step. Perhaps I'm being creepy here? I don't know. I try seeing this from her eyes – what will she think when she sees me at her door, uninvited and unexpected? A pleasant surprise or perhaps not. She might think me sinister; she might think I'm one of those guys that go about stalking women. She is an incredibly attractive woman, after all. I slow down as I approach her

house. A woman walking her small dog passes by. The dog
stops and cocks its leg against a tree. The woman and I nod at
each other. And now I am here, outside Alice's house, and I
have to fight the urge to turn around and head straight back
to the safety of the barber shop. But I know I cannot. This is
exactly the sort of situation I need to tackle head-on, I need to
'man up', as they say. I need to stop running away. But I still
take my phone out from my back pocket and scroll through
to Alice's mobile number. My finger hovers above it, ready to
tap the number, ready to take the easy way out. No, I have to
do this. I return the phone to my pocket.

I walk up to the front door and there's a number of buzzers.
Alice's is number two, the first floor. I hit the buzzer and wait,
hoping she isn't in. I buzz a second time. It takes a fair while
but eventually her voice comes across the tinny speaker, loud
and clear: 'Who is it?'

'Oh, hi, yes. It's, erm, Mac…'

'Mac?'

'From the Mac the Clipper. I wonder–'

'Do you wanna come up?'

'Sure, if it's not a bad time or anything.'

The buzzer buzzes. I push the door and I'm in. I pick up
the post and a free newspaper on the doormat and leave them
on the stairs. There's a letter addressed to Alice but somehow
the thought of handing it to her would make me look even
more creepy. A ginger cat comes up to greet me. A friendly
little thing. It purrs and I stroke it, and somehow this simple
action calms me a little. I walk up the stairs, up to the first
floor. Everything is neat and clean. It's a well looked after
house. Her door is slightly ajar. I tap on it quietly. 'Hello?'

'Hi, come in.'

And here she is, standing in front of me in her small hallway.

I think my knees are about to give way. She is so beautiful, with her blonde hair cascading down, her eyes, so full of life, staring into mine, and those lips that so need kissing.

Chapter 4: Alice

I ring my mother in Keswick with my news – I've got a new job! I tell her about my interviews with Mac at Mac the Clipper and Ian at Top Cutz, with a 'z'. Somehow, I didn't get the job with Mac and I'm so disappointed. It was to do with the fact I couldn't give him a reference from my last boss. How could I? The way he tried it on with me and the way he fired me when I pushed him off, the bastard. Perhaps it's a good thing Mac didn't give me the job – how could I work with a man like that as my boss day in, day out, while having entirely inappropriate thoughts about him? The man's too gorgeous to be my boss. But I know how to behave, I would never push him against a wall as my ex-boss did. Problem is, I wasn't too taken with Ian. He also came across as rather sleazy, and I worry he gave me the job for the wrong reasons. Still, I can't tell my mother this so I just tell her I'm delighted.

'Why don't you come home, love?' she says. 'Get yourself a job up here.'

'Oh, Mum. I know you miss me and I miss you, and one day I'll come back but…'

'I know.' I hear her sigh. 'You've been dazzled by all those bright lights, haven't you?'

'Well, yeah, London's great, Mum. And it's nice for Gran to have someone nearby who can pop in to say hello to her occasionally.'

'Any news on the boyfriend front yet?'

'No, Mum, there's no news *on the boyfriend front*,' I say, impersonating her Lake District accent. She launches into her *better not leave it too long* lecture and *You're not getting any younger*, etc, etc. Thankfully, I'm saved by the door buzzer, which, in itself, is a rare thing: I don't get many visitors, having not long been here in this flat. 'Mum, I've got to go; someone's at the door.'

She carries on talking as if she hadn't heard. Who could be calling me? I'm not expecting anyone. I'm not sure I like this. Eventually, I manage to get rid of my mother, bless her. The buzzer rings a second time. 'Who is it?' I ask through the intercom.

'Oh, hi, yes. It's, erm, Mac…'

'Mac?' My heart thuds. Mac? Here?

'From the Mac the Clipper. I wonder–'

Shit, what does he want? 'Do you wanna come up?' I blurt out.

'Sure, if it's not a bad time or anything.' I press the button, allowing him in.

I leave the flat door ajar and rush into the bathroom and check my appearance in the mirror. It's too late to apply a fresh layer of make-up but I don't look too shabby. I undo a couple of buttons on my blouse. Puffing out my cheeks, I step back into the hallway, and there he is.

'I wasn't expecting this,' I say as he steps dinside, a smile on his lips. Gee, he is so darn attractive. Does he know it? Does he know what sort of effect he has on me? I mean, Christ, this doesn't happen every day, not like this. He must have a queue of women waiting outside his door.

I invite him in. He declines the coffee I offer him. It's a small kitchen, but tidy, everything in its place, dark green cupboards, and a small dining table with a Formica top. There's a framed print of Van Gogh's sunflowers on the wall. I hope he approves. I remain on my feet, leaning against the sink, the afternoon sun shining through the window behind me. 'I thought I gave you my number,' I say, more curtly than I'd intended.

'Yeah, I know. I tried it a few times but it must have been switched off or something.'

'Oh yes, actually I think you're right. So…' I take a deep breath. 'I'm guessing this is a professional call, not… a personal one.'

'Yeah, that's right. Thanks for coming over earlier. It was nice to meet you. So, fact is, Alice, I wondered… I mean, I wanted to offer you the job.'

Shit! I didn't expect that. I assumed I hadn't got it. 'Really?'

'It's yours if you want it.'

'Right.' Wow. Not sure how to proceed here. 'I've gotta be honest, I wasn't expecting that. I thought…'

'I know. It didn't give you an easy ride. I'm sorry about that. Well? Would you like the job?'

I shake my head. 'I would have, yeah, for sure. I would have loved it. But you know I told you–'

'You had an interview at Top Cutz.'

'With Ian, yeah. Well, fact is, I'd barely walked through the door and he offered me the job.'

'Oh, right. OK.'

He looks genuinely disappointed. 'Yeah, I'm… I'm sorry.'

'No, that's fine. That's good then, that's… that's excellent.'

'Yeah. Yes, it is.'

A silence drops between us. There's no point in him being here a moment longer; he knows that, we both know that, yet I don't want him to leave. 'When… when do you s-start?' he asks.

'Tomorrow.'

'Well, I'm sure you'll be very happy there. Ian runs a decent barbershop. Not as good as mine though,' he adds with a smile.

'No.'

'You know, you could still come work for me; you're allowed to change your mind.'

'Er…' It's true, I could but I've already said yes to Ian and the old-fashioned part of me wants to honour that. Also, I'm not sure my heart could take working for Mac, knowing he was always around, so close but utterly untouchable. 'I'm sorry, I couldn't. Call me old-fashioned but–'

'No, it's fine.' He puts his hands up. 'I'm sorry, I shouldn't have said that. It's not fair to put you on the spot.'

'But if it all goes tits up, I know where to go.'

'Yeah, absolutely. I'm sorry I…'

'It's OK. Really, it's all right.'

'It's a nice flat you've got. How long have you lived here?'

'About six months. So, yeah, the rent's not cheap but I manage - just about - and, as you say, it's a lovely flat and a really nice area. I feel safe around here. Some good barbers too, so I'm told.'

'For sure. There's one, in particular, that is the best in all of North London.'

'And some swell guys that work there.'

He clicks his fingers at me. 'That's the one.'

I laugh. We amble towards the flat door. 'Thanks for taking the time to come see me, Mac. I appreciate it. I'm sorry it didn't work out.'

'Yeah. So am I.'

We stand at the door and I feel the heaviness of the situation, the words that remain unsaid between us. But he came in in a professional capacity, we just can't jump from one to the other. The risk is too big. What if I'm imagining it all, that this mutual longing isn't mutual at all, and that it's just me, projecting my desires, my needs, onto this poor man. I swallow.

I open the door for him. 'Might see you around some point.'

'Yeah, sure. You know where we are. Just pop in and say hi. Anytime.'

'Yeah, sure. I might well do that.'

'Goodbye, Alice, and thanks anyway.'

'It's fine. No problem. Bye, Mac.'

I close the door on him and I'm left standing in my small hallway, not sure whether to laugh or cry, not sure whether to chase after him and tell him I've changed my mind, that, yes, I do want to work for him, I do, I do, and so much more. I wonder what he's thinking right this moment. I go through to the bedroom and flop onto the bed, my emotions all over the place, wondering whether I'd ever see him again.

Chapter 5: Mac

Sunny Grove, Dad's care home, isn't too far away. I take the car; about the only time I ever use it. It usually takes me fifteen minutes to drive there. The staff know me by now. I usually go to visit twice a week, one evening after work and, if I can face it, every Sunday. I feel guilty even about that – is it enough? Should I visit more often? But I run my own business and I work full time. I get tired, and visiting Father is always a draining affair. Some days his mind will be sharp and he'll recognise me and we can actually have a conversation, nothing very deep or interesting but a conversation, nonetheless. But sadly most days, he'll not recognise me and he'll ask who I am or not even say anything. It doesn't help that I have to wear a face mask the whole time I'm in the home. Then, I just sit next to him, pat his hand occasionally, say the odd word which he'll not hear or not understand, and that'll be it.

My mother deserted us when I was still a kid. I was nine years old. I've not seen or heard from her since. Not once, not a single word. And even now, after all this time and as a grown man, it hurts; it bloody hurts. Why did she leave? It's something I ask myself every day, every single day, and have done so since that very first day so long ago. I'd ask Dad. 'Where is she, Dad? Where has she gone? Why did she leave us, Dad?' Why, why, why? Did she not have any sense of loyalty to us, to my father, to her nine-year-old son? Obviously not. My mother had no loyalty to anyone – except perhaps herself.

The care home is two large Edwardian houses merged into one. It accommodates about fifteen residents. It's a Tuesday evening; the ground is still wet after an earlier downpour, and the air smells fresh. I press the buzzer next to the front door and the door swings open. I walk in and breathe in the familiar smell of disinfectant and canteen-like food. One of the carers greets me as she passes. I walk through to the lounge area. A number of residents, mostly female, sit around the perimeter, some vaguely watching the mounted television set that is permanently switched on, all day, every day. Father isn't here. I walk through to the conservatory and find him sitting alone in an armchair staring out into the garden, watching a robin pecking at a bird feeder swinging from a low branch of the elm tree. He has a mug of something in his hand, and a plate on the little table next to him, empty save for a couple of tell-tale crumbs.

'Hello, Dad.'

'Hmm? Who's that?'

'Your son.' I pull up a hardback chair and sit next to him. 'How are you today?' He pulls his red cardigan tighter; he smells of carbolic soap. 'Have you had your lunch?'

'Oh yes.' He proceeds to tell me in great detail what he ate for lunch. Anyone listening would have thought he'd eaten at the Ritz. It's all nonsense, of course. He brushes away some crumbs from his corduroy trousers.

'So, you're Thomas, aren't you?'

'Yes, Dad.' My name is actually Thomas McIntosh, but people call me Mac.

'How old are you now?'

'Twenty-nine, Dad. Almost at the Big Three-Oh.'

He nods. 'A nice age, a nice age.'

My father often asks about people's ages. If I ask him how old he is, the answer varies from twenty-five to forty depending on where he is in the recesses of his memory at that particular moment. He is never older than forty.

A carer called Patsy, according to her name badge, with a face mask and a swirly tattoo around her wrist pops in and offers me a tea. I thank her but say no. I won't be staying long; I rarely do.

Another resident wanders in holding a cup and saucer. Mrs Charlton stoops, wears a beige skirt and jacket with a large, kingfisher brooch. She looks dapper. She dresses the same every day. She looks like she's got an important meeting to go to. But she hasn't. She simply walks around the care home all day, taking delight in seeing things or people for what she thinks is the first time when, of course, she has seen them a thousand times already. 'Aha, Mr McIntosh, there you are,' she says to my father as if she'd been genuinely looking for him. The cup tilts on the saucer. 'Soon be time for tea. I hope you're hungry.'

'Go away, you old bat,' says Dad.

'Hello, Mrs Charlton,' I say to her.

'Hello there. And you are…?'

We've met several times before but I smile and tell her. 'I'm Thomas, Mr McIntosh's son. Nice to meet you.'

Satisfied with this, she about-turns and ambles back the way she came, cup and saucer at a precarious angle.

So, I tell my father what I've been doing the last few days. Sometimes, like today, he listens intently, and he says something or asks a question which shows he's been listening and understanding everything I've said. Other times, he'll say something totally random and unrelated, and it's as if he's not heard a word, or taken anything in. I carry on talking while my father waits for another bird to appear and take its turn at the feeder. I tell him all about Alice and her interview, and my visit to her flat, and what an absolute tool I've been.

He pats me on the knee and says, 'You were an idiot for a reason.'

'What?'

'Your heart was protecting you.'

My mouth drops: it's been years since I've heard my father utter such an articulate sentence. 'What do you mean, *protecting* me?'

'You don't need a woman in your life, son. Waste of time. Love them and leave them, if you want, but whatever you do, son, don't ever fall for one. Because she'll be the death of you.'

OK, I need to tread carefully here. 'Like my mum, you mean.'

'Your mother was a bitch.'

Ow, my mouth drops open, did he just say that? Did he actually just call my mother that word? I feel as if he's just punched me in the stomach. I can't believe it. I know Mum left him, and me, I know it must have hurt like crazy but how could he have used such a foul, horrible word? 'That's a bit harsh, Dad.'

'She was.' He folds his arms across his chest. 'Bitch.'

'Alice's not left me, Dad. We don't even know each other yet.' I stop at my use of the word *yet*. Why did I say that? The chances are, I'll never see her again. The thought of it pulls at my heart. 'Why did Mum leave, Dad?' There we are, I ask again…

But he looks confused again. I've lost him. 'Where is that robin?' He points outside. 'Look, he's back.'

'Who's back? Oh, yes. Mr Robin. Of course.'

'We have a bird table in the garden. I put breadcrumbs on it every day.'

I've heard this several times, this inconsequential reference back to his childhood said in the present tense. Now, comes the part about his father…

'I sit in the garden for hours sometimes. Best place to escape my dad. He's got a temper on him, that man. Best to lay low, avoid him, you know?'

'You like the birds, don't you, Dad?' I look at my phone, it's time to go, otherwise I'll tire him out. He can only cope with short visits. 'Well, Dad,' I say, standing up. 'I'd better be going. Good to see you again.' (Even if you did call my mother a bitch). 'I'll come by again soon, if that's OK.'

'He will get fat.'

I look out at the robin. 'Yes, you're right,' I say. 'Very fat.'

As I leave, I see Mrs Charlton again, still with her cup and saucer precariously tilted. I flash her a smile but she doesn't notice.

I sit in my car, a little rust-coloured Peugeot, and sigh. Why did I bother? Who benefits from my visits? Was it just to show the staff I was a caring, loving son? But we keep going, don't we?

Chapter 6: Mac

The White Oak pub is already brimming by the time we roll up at nine. The music is loud, the customers drunk and the atmosphere buzzing. We get our drinks and dance a little. We always attract some attention, too much most of the time. I guess we make a striking trio. Until recently, we were a quartet but of course that was before Jack jumped ship and deserted us like the rat that he is. Three big, broad men with big beards and covered with tattoos. Eoin and Tony also have several piercings between them and perhaps in places I'd rather not think about! I, however, do not. I've nothing against piercings myself but they're not for me! We know how to drink, the three of us. And because of our size, we usually drink an awful lot, far more than is good for us, for it takes quite a few pints before we begin to feel the slightest effect. But it's the fact we come in together, the three of us, that attracts such an audience. Some people think we're gay, three hairy men together, dressed much the same, same attitude, same vibe. Now, I'm no homophobe, trust me, but no one calls me gay to my face. We get even more attention from the ladies who, sometimes, think we're some sort of strip act. When I tell them we simply cut hair for a living, it's always a bit of a surprise and maybe a disappointment, I don't know. Women have been known to throw themselves at us. Eoin and Tony enjoy it, but that's not me, not my style. I'm no angel, I've had my fair share of one-night stands, especially when I was younger, but now that I'm almost thirty, it doesn't appeal so much, and I hate that feeling of post-coital emptiness that comes with it.

Tonight I'm not in the mood for talking. This business with Alice and what my father said about my mother is bothering me. All I want to do is dance and drink, to let the music take over, to lose myself and drown my woes in several pints of lager. Eoin and Tony know I need space; they let me be, just check up on me every now and then. I wish Jack was here. Jack was the most empathic of the gang; I could have spoken to Jack and he would have listened, and he would have known what to say. I miss him. I miss him very much.

Tony and Eoin are playing pool and chatting to a couple of girls. There's much laughter coming from that corner of the pub. I head to the bar to get another drink. I'm just paying when the door opens and there's Ian with a couple of his mates in tow. The place seems to go silent for a few moments; it's like a scene out of a Western – the bad guy comes through the swinging saloon doors, his thumbs hooked into his belt, and surveys the scene before him. Conversations stop, card games cease, the men gulp, the women breathe in and push up their hair. The good guy is sitting on a stool at the bar. The two men clock each other and finger their revolvers.

Ian spots me straight away. He saunters over, a swagger in his step. I guess he has a lot to feel pleased about: he'd stolen my friend from me and he'd bagged the girl.

'Alright, Mac,' he says with a wink. His two mates prop up

the bar behind him.

'Yeah.'

He orders himself and his mates a round of drinks. He doesn't offer to get me one, not that I need one; I'd just got myself a fresh pint, and somehow accepting a drink off this man would feel wrong.

'Jack's settling in well,' he says, sipping his drink. 'The lad's doing well. He's good at his job. You must be gutted he left you, Mac. Gutted. I know I'd be. What did you do, Mac? Made a pass at him or something?' He laughs.

'Yeah, right.'

'And now the lovely Alice has started with us. Christ, what a stunner she is. I would have thought better of you, Mac, letting her slip through your grubby little fingers. I reckon you're losing your touch, mate.'

'I hope they'll both be very happy at yours,' I say before taking my drink and moving back to my table with the boys. I have no desire to stay talking to Ian.

But Ian can never resist a gloat for too long, and having started, he wants to gloat some more. So, he comes over with his stupid grin, and starts talking to Tony and Eoin. You can see by their body language that neither are happy about this. Then I hear Ian challenge Eoin to a darts match. I shake my head, don't do it, Eoin, don't accept. He accepts, damn him. So they walk over towards the darts board and chalk up their names and choose their darts. Ian's making a big thing of this, taking far too long over it. And I know why – he wants to attract an audience, wants people to witness him winning. Ian always needs to be the Big Man. And I know he's good at darts and he'll wipe the floor with Eoin. But maybe Eoin doesn't realise this because I see money exchanging hands – quite a bit. Tony catches my eye and shakes his head. Maybe Eoin's had too much to drink already and it's messed up his self-control. Eoin likes to hold onto his money so what's he playing at?

By now a sizable crowd has indeed gathered around to watch Ian thrash Eoin at darts. Ian's mates are among them.

They begin, and people cheer and applaud every move. The music's turned down, this has now become the focal point of the whole pub. Amazingly, Eoin is doing well and is surging ahead. He might win this. My anticipation rises a notch. It's only a silly game of darts but boy, do I want him to win, to beat the arrogant, strutting Ian. Ian seems to be missing his targets – always by a whisker. And then, almost at the end of the contest, with Eoin some distance ahead, I realise what's happening. Ian's doing this on purpose. He's letting Eoin win. We're almost at the end; Eoin just needs a 'double eighteen' to win, and he's got three darts to play. He misses the first, and the crowd 'oo's'; he misses the second by some distance, and the crowd 'ahh's', but then, with his final dart – double eighteen. Eoin throws his arms up in the air, he's delighted, the crowd holler and cheer.

Ian shakes Eoin's hand and this is where I'll see if I'm right, whether Ian threw the game on purpose. I move in closer and so I hear them talking.

'So, how about it, Eoin? You feeling lucky? Double bet this time or, if you like, even treble?'

Eoin barely hesitates, too flushed by his victory to see that Ian's playing him. 'Sure,' he says loudly. 'Why not. Treble bet.' He has no idea he's stepping into Ian's trap. Ian puts out his hand and Eoin is about to take it. The crowd cheer, keen to see another game with a fair amount of money riding on it.

'No,' I shout, stepping forward. 'Don't shake.'

Everyone's eyes turn towards me.

'Eoin, mate,' I say. 'Quit while you're ahead. You don't need to play this.'

'Sod off, Mac,' says Ian. 'This is none of your business.'

'No one likes a scammer, Ian.'

One could hear the collective gasp. 'Who said anything about a scammer.'

I step right up to him. He's a good couple inches shorter than me. 'I know what you're up to, Ian, so back off.'

Eoin's voice cuts through. 'Mac, it's all right, mate. I beat him once; I can do it again.'

'That's what he wants you to think, can't you see that?' But he can't; he's too high on winning and alcohol.

'It's all right, Mac.'

Ian whispers, 'If you're so concerned for your friend here, why don't you take his place?'

I think about this. Could I beat Ian? I'm better at darts than Eoin, but as good as Ian? Possibly. I wasn't sure.

'But not double,' he says loudly so that everyone can hear. 'Not treble but quadruple.'

A cheer goes up. I look at Eoin. He's looking worried now. 'OK,' I say, not quite believing I'm saying it. 'You're on.'

Another cheer.

The pub falls quiet. The music is turned off entirely. It's apparent from the off that Ian is a good player, much better against me than he was against Eoin. This may surprise everyone else in the room, but it doesn't surprise me. We start off level-pegging but then I make a couple of errors. I curse myself. The more I concentrate, the more pressure I feel, and the less well I play. In no time, Ian is surging ahead. He gets so far ahead, I know I won't be able to catch up; I will only win if Ian cocks up dramatically, and somehow, I can't see that happening. The crowd is anticipating Ian's win, and they don't have to wait too long. Ian finishes with a flourish, getting a 'double fifteen' on his first try. The money, every damn last penny of it, is his. The crowd cheers, holding their drinks up in the air. I give Ian his winnings.

Ian offers me his hand. Reluctantly, I take it. To ignore it would only make me appear churlish and a bad loser. 'Another time, eh, mate?' he says with a wink. I could happily punch him. 'Well, they say bad luck comes in threes.'

He tips the brim of an invisible hat and joins his mates. I, in turn, sidle up to Tony and Eoin. 'I can't believe that just happened,' says Eoin.

Tony slaps Eoin on the back. 'So much for the luck of the Irish! He let you win on purpose, didn't he, so he could clean up second time round. Oldest trick in the book, mate.'

'I owe you, Mac,' says Eoin.

'No you don't. Don't worry about it.'

He looks shifty. I catch him raising his eyebrows at Tony.

'You can buy me a drink if it helps,' I say.

He nods. 'Sure, Mac.'

*

Another couple of hours pass. The three of us have had a few drinks each; we're happy; we're the very best of mates – at work and out of it. The Three Musketeers. Not the same as the Four Musketeers but that's Jack's loss.

I'm washing my hands in the toilet when Ian comes in. 'Hey, Mac,' he says. I look up to the mirror and see him. His face is flushed. He also has had a drink or two too many. 'Good night tonight, wasn't it?'

I don't bother answering.

'This Alice woman. Can't wait to see her again. And I still can't believe you let her go. I mean, what a woman. God, the woman's sex on legs, did you clock the size of her breasts, Mac? God, it makes a man go weak at the knees, I'm telling you.'

I put my hands under the dryer while Ian stands at the urinal. 'Yeah, whatever, just, maybe, don't talk about her like that.'

'What?' he shouts over the air dryer.

'I said show some fucking respect.'

He finishes and is zipping himself up, looking at me. 'You what? Show her some respect? Sure, I will, man, but I'd like to show her much more than just my respect.' He laughs, and I hate him for his crudeness. Yes, I fancied her too, yes, she did something to me, but I would never, ever talk about a woman like that. Again, I want to punch the bastard, but I hold onto myself. I'm drunk, I know I am, and I know if I hit him, I'd be liable to lose control of myself, and I'd be taking out my failures on him. I step out of the toilet, not wanting to see Ian a moment longer, not trusting myself.

It was me that lost Jack, it was me that lost Alice, it was me that lost a shed load of money in a stupid game of darts. Ian may be a lowlife of a man but I'm the failure here, I'm the one responsible for my own cockups. Ian can try to hurt me as much as he likes with his cheap words and cruel taunts but no one can hurt me as much as I can hurt myself.

*

I'm on my way home. The boys and I often go out like this. We meet up in the White Oak, we have a few drinks and a good laugh, then head home, but tonight, I've drunk too much, far too much. I know why. I've let Ian rile me. I should be bigger than this, stronger. Turns out I'm not, I'm as petty and as weak as anyone else.

It's late, almost midnight, and I've got to open up shop tomorrow morning so I really ought to be heading home but instead, I've made a small detour and I find myself outside Alice's house. The lights are off, she'll be tucked up in bed looking forward to her day of work in a barber's shop tomorrow. If it wasn't for my irrational fears and stupid prejudices, she would have been coming to my shop, to work with me. Over the years, I've allowed my father's hurt to become my hurt. The woman he loved, the woman he was devoted to, upped and left and it ruined his life forever. We all know history can repeat itself, and I must guard against that. People see the big bloke I am on the outside, they see the beard and the muscles and the tattoos, but they don't see the delicate heart that beats within. It's a mild night. I could stay here for hours standing in the street, looking up at Alice's window like some lovelorn Romeo. But I need to go.

Halfway home, I take a short cut down Jack's road and now I find myself standing outside his house. He's got a decent flat on the second floor, lives by himself. He had a girlfriend until recently but, for whatever reasons, they split up. His light's still on and I can actually see him up there passing by his window. I pick up a tiny stone from the pavement and throw it up at his window. It misses. My second attempt hits. He comes to the window and peers out. He doesn't see me. He opens his window, an old-fashioned sash window, and leans out. I call his name.

It takes him a second to recognise my voice. 'Mac, is that you?'

I step out from the shadows of the pavement and onto the road.

'What the fuck, Mac?'

'So, how's it going, Jack, with Ian and his shop? Is it worth it, eh? That little, tiny bit of extra pay? Does it make up for shafting your mates?'

People in other houses and other flats are drawing open their curtains, opening their windows, wondering what all the noise is about.

Jack's not happy with me. 'Fuck off, Mac, you don't come round here in the middle of the night and bollock me. People leave jobs all the time, they move on. It's life, Mac, so grow up and get used to it.'

'It's more than a job, we were mates, a gang, you know that.'

Someone tells me to shut up, another tells me to fuck off, another warns me they're calling the police.

'Go home, Mac. You're drunk. Go home now.' He slams the window down and a moment later his flat goes black as he switches off his lights.

I'm in the middle of a road looking like an utter fool. A taxi comes hurtling towards me, an electric one. I don't hear it until the last moment. It beeps its horn at me. I jump out of the way, my heart beating hard as the car whooshes by.

It's time to go home.

Chapter 7: Mac

One week later

It's that time of week when I visit my father. It's early evening, the sun fading, the shadows long. I step into the care home, my face mask on, when the manager of the place, Mrs Hale, jumps out at me. 'Ah, Mr MacIntosh. I was hoping to see you. Can I have a quick word before you go see your father?'

'Sure,' I say, not liking the sound of this one bit. 'Is there anything wrong?'

She pulls a face. 'Not wrong as such but we are concerned. Your father has his ups and downs as you know, like all of us, but he's been particularly down this last day or two. I wanted to wait to see whether there was any improvement before I contacted you and sadly there hasn't been. He hasn't spoken a word for almost three days now, and, more worryingly, he's not eating and hardly drinking. He's dehydrated but refusing to do anything about it. It's not a big concern yet so no need for doctors at this point but we are keeping a careful eye on him. I wanted to alert you before you go in and see him.'

'OK, I see. Well, thank you, Mrs Hale.'

I find Dad as usual in the conservatory staring out into the garden. I wonder if he's waiting for the robin again. He does look pale and weaker even compared to a week ago. He has visibly deteriorated and the sight of him makes my heart ache. 'Hi, Dad, how's it going?'

He looks up at me and I can see for myself that this is not a good day – his eyes look clouded and he definitely doesn't recognise me. I pat the back of his hand and draw a chair up and sit next to him. 'Has the robin appeared?'

'Robin who?'

'No, I mean the bird, Dad. Last time you were…' I know this is a pointless conversation. 'Dad, Mrs Hale says you're not eating and she's concerned for you. She says you're dehydrated.'

He doesn't answer nor look at me. There's a glass of water on the table next to him. I pass it to him but, still without looking at me, simply shakes his head. He doesn't want it. I put the glass back down and sigh.

What I really want to know is what he meant last week when he called my mother a bitch. I hated him for saying that, and it's been bugging me all week. I can understand it, in truth, his wife walking out on him, leaving him with a young child to look after and bring up by himself, must've been so hard but still, 'bitch' is such a harsh, unforgiving word, and hearing him say it brought out a protective streak in me, I wanted to protect the very woman I've not seen since I was nine years old and had hurt me so much. Not a day goes by when I don't at some point wonder what happened to her. Every day, I ask, why did you leave us, Mum? Why? Whether she was still alive even, whether she met someone knew and started again. Did she have more children, do I have half brothers or sisters somewhere? Surely, she would have let me know, she wouldn't keep such a thing from me. But who knows, she was hard-hearted enough to leave me without a bye or a leave, she has to be capable of anything.

So, I resign myself to sitting with Dad as if I was a total stranger to him. We could be fellow travellers on an underground train, sitting next to each other for a few minutes, ignoring each other, then the train will pull in at my station and I'll get up, vacate my seat and exit the train, and the man next to me will not give me a second thought.

'I've not seen that nice woman since. You know, the one I was telling you about the other day, Alice?'

He doesn't answer, not a flicker of acknowledgement. It shouldn't matter but the total lack of communication somehow hurts.

Time passes slowly. I check the time on my phone numerous times. Patsy, the carer with a swirly tattoo around her wrist offers me a cup of tea. I smile behind my mask and say no thanks. After a while, I decide to leave. It's not been a good visit; my father has not said a single word to me and has kept his attention entirely focused on the garden outside. I feel rather depressed by it all. I pat his hand again and stand up. 'Oh well, Dad. I'll see in a few days, OK? Look after yourself.' He still doesn't answer. 'Dad, please try and eat something. You *need* to get something down you. Please, Dad.'

Please acknowledge, please look at me, even if it's just for a second. He does not, and I leave with a pebble in my heart.

To leave the care home from the conservatory, one has to pass through the dining room. As I pass, I see Mrs Charlton sitting at one of the tables, and she also has a visitor, whose back is turned to me. I stop in my tracks – that hair, the colour of it, the way it falls down over her shoulders, Jesus, it looks like Alice from behind. But it can't be, surely, not here of all places? Yet I'm sure it's her. My heart speeds up, my mouth turns dry. All I need to do is step round and I'll see for myself but I'm rooted to the spot. Mrs Charlton, wearing her beige jacket with its kingfisher brooch, becomes aware of my brooding presence. She looks over at me and, perhaps recognizing me, smiles. Her visitor shifts in her chair and turns around. Oh my god, it's her!

'A-Alice,' I blurt out. 'My god, what are you… I mean, hello.'

She laughs. 'Why, hello, Mac, didn't expect to see you here either.'

We stare at each other and my heart is about ready to burst. I thought she was beautiful but somehow her beauty had dimmed over the last week. Now, seeing her again, her beauty is overwhelming me, the gleam in her eyes, the pale perfection of her skin, her lips and her cupid bow… Then, we both snap out of our wordless gaze. 'Oh, Gran,' she says. 'Sorry. This is…' She turns back to me. 'My friend Mac.'

'We've met before,' I say, stepping forward, offering my hand.

She ignores my outstretched hand. 'Is that your father in the conservatory?' she asks. 'The grumpy one.'

'Gran!' shrieks Alice. 'You can't say that.'

I laugh. 'To be fair, he is rather grumpy. Especially today, for some reason.'

'Nonetheless, Gran.' Turning to me, she adds, 'I'm sure he's very nice, your father.'

'He has his moments but today's not a good day for him. You know what it's like.'

She flashes a smile of recognition. 'Yes. I do.'

She's wearing a pleated blue skirt and a black sleeveless top, exposing the gentle smattering of freckles on her forearms. I so want to speak to her but feel as if I can't interrupt her time with her grandmother. 'Well, anyway, it was nice to see you again…'

She stands for some reason. 'Yeah, you too, Mac.'

And I know there's something we could say here, I can see it in her eyes, but instead, I bow ever so slightly and back away.

With a heavy heart, I return to my car, parked outside in the street. The day is overcast now, as grey as my mood. I sit at the wheel, the key in the ignition but I can't bring myself to drive away. Alice is in there, in the home, and again I'm running away. I should go back in there and speak to her properly, ask her out, make my intentions clear. But I can't. I can't impose myself while she is spending time with her grandmother, it'd be totally inappropriate. So I remain in my car. I hit the steering wheel in frustration. I buckle my seatbelt and turn on the ignition. I check my rear-view mirror and my every sense stills – there she is, crossing the road, buttoning her coat, her car keys in her hand. I watch as she approaches her car, a red-coloured Ford Fiesta, unlocking it from a distance.

This is it, I say to myself. Don't think about it; it'll be too late. Just do it, just act now.

I jump out of the car, calling her name. She stops and turns around. Her eyes widen on seeing me. 'Mac?'

'Alice.'

'You OK?'

'Yes. No. I mean, the thing is, Alice…'

'Would you care to meet up, Mac? A drink perhaps?'

'Oh? Wow, yes, I mean, yes.'

She laughs. 'There's a new bar on the high street. Called Celsius. Shall we say eight tonight?'

I can hardly speak. 'Yeah, yeah,' I blurt out like an idiot. 'Eight at Celsius. Sure. Brilliant.'

She flashes me a wide smile. 'See you then,' she says with a little wave, turning back in the direction of her car.

I return to my car. I slam the door shut and watch Alice drive away down the street. It's only as she disappears around the corner that I scream with happiness.

*

I return to the shop with a skip in my step while at the same feeling a sense of dread. It'd been an exhausting visit to the care home, the joy of seeing Alice in sharp contrast to seeing my father in such a weakened state. It's good to get back to the sanctuary of my shop. Both Eoin and Tony are busy with customers and there's a queue of people waiting, two of them wearing black face masks. I say hello to all the customers, most of whom I know as returning customers. I have a quick catch-up with the boys. All's well although Eoin says we got a phone call on the shop's landline. 'Some woman asking for our email address.'

'We don't have one.'

'Well, yeah, I know that. She wanted to write an email to you specifically, Mac, that's why she didn't want to use our Instagram or Facebook or anything, just email.'

'What have you been up to, eh, Mac?' says Tony 'Your past catching up with you?'

'So, hope you don't mind, mate, I gave her your email address.'

'Did she say her name?'

'Nope. I asked but she refused. Just said she'd email you.'

'All right. Cheers, mate.'

I check my email on my phone but there's nothing there

45

that shouldn't be there, just a whole lot of junk and various newsletters I never read but never get round to unsubscribing. It doesn't matter. Far more important – I've got a date tonight, a hot date with a hot woman, and I'm nervous, terrified and excited all at the same time. I turn to my customers with a smile. 'Right then, who's next?'

Chapter 8: Alice

'So, how's it going at Top Cutz?' Mac asks me.

I take a large sip of my white wine and nod but the words don't come.

'That good?' he asks.

'Yeah! No, it's going well. I mean, it's only been a week but I'm enjoying it. It's busy, the customers are good, generally.'

'Generally?'

I draw a deep breath. 'There's some rough ones, I have to say. They make comments about me, you know.'

'Geez, I'm sorry to hear that.'

'It's OK, I can handle it. I think they quite enjoy the put-downs, it's like a banter to them. But it gets wearing after a while.'

'Doesn't Ian help out?'

'I don't need his help.' Did that sound too harsh?

'I know but they're his customers though.'

'We're reaching an understanding.'

So, here we are, just gone eight on a Tuesday evening in this new, trendy north London bar called Celsius, full of hipsters, like us, I guess, and London's trendy young things. The place is busy, the music already loud. There's a group of four girls dancing to Avicii on the small dance floor. Mac and I sit on padded seats in a semi-circular booth. I've come in a figure-hugging red skirt with an eighties-style split up one side, and an equally figure-hugging yellow blouse with large, daisy-shaped buttons, showing a hint of my lace-edged bra beneath. I'm hoping it's having some sort of effect on him.

'How is Ian?' he asks.

'He's fine, he's very nice. Considerate.'

'*Considerate*? Ian?'

He obviously sees through my lie. But I don't want Mac thinking I've made a mistake so I plough on: 'He's a good boss, he's teaching me lots about men's hair. His customers like him. I like him. There's more to him than meets the eye, you know. The fact he's rather good-looking helps.'

Did I imagine it or did Mac sneer a little at that? I think so. I hope so. He doesn't say anything and instead sips his lager. I gulp my wine, a little flushed. 'Ian's better than my previous boss. It was a hairdresser but the boss was a man and…'

'You don't have to say it.'

'Let's just say, he took *too much* of a shine to me, you know? It was awkward. So, I left and he refused to give me a reference. That's why…'

'I see. I'm sorry.'

'It's OK.'

'And how's Jack?' he asks.

'Yeah, he's cool. I like him. He started the day before me. I think he's missing you guys but he's doing OK.'

He shakes his head. 'I still don't know why he left. I mean, the four of us are more than just barbers, we're the best of mates. We've been together for years and suddenly Jack jumps ship.'

'He can still be friends with you, can't he?'

'Yes, I suppose but no, he broke something. I wouldn't have minded if he'd gone somewhere far away but to go to Ian's and Top Cutz? That hurt, Alice.'

'I feel bad for going there myself now.'

'No, that's different. You weren't to know.'

'And I didn't jump ship, Mac. You pushed me.'

He takes a drink. 'Yeah.'

The girls, still dancing, have been joined by a couple of lads now, dancing to Bruno Mars, their arms in the air. How happy they all look. I look at Mac who's also watching them, sipping his drink, desperately wondering how to bring this round, how to break this impasse that's developed here.

But somehow I only manage to make it worse. I turn to him and, leaning forward, ask, 'What did I do wrong, Mac? Why didn't you want me for your shop until it was too late? It wasn't really about men's hair, was it? I felt as if it was something else, something I said, maybe.'

'No, not at all, it was nothing you said, Alice.'

He looks so sad all of a sudden that I have to fight the desire to reach out and take his hand. 'So what was it then?'

'I was worried, Alice. Worried that a woman would upset the dynamic. I was wrong, I see that now. I'm sorry.'

'I'm sorry too. I would have worked for you in a shot.'

'You could...' He speaks slowly, 'You could still come work for me... if you like.'

I shake my head. 'No, it's too late now.'

'Is it? Why?'

I glance away for a moment. Then, returning my gaze to him, I say, 'You should never work for someone you fancy.'

Chapter 9: Mac

The world seems to stop on its axis at that moment, the music seems to fade, the dancers blur. The way Alice looks into my eyes, I can see her desire for me, slightly faltering perhaps, unsure whether she has said too much, an uncertain smile on her lips. 'No,' I say. 'You're right, you should never work for someone you fancy, nor should one employ someone you fancy.' I reach my hand across the table and take her hand. She leans towards me. We kiss, the gentlest of kisses, a nervous, hesitant kiss. My cock stirs into life. Yet, as soon as the kiss is over, I want more. We kiss again, my cock hardening, the music swirling around us.

She smiles at me. 'I've been wanting to do that from the first moment I saw you.'

'Me too. I have thought about nothing but you, Alice. It's been unbearable.'

She laughs. 'I'm sorry.'

'It doesn't matter now.'

'I feel the same. I can't get you out of my head, Mac. I wake up and you're there! You won't leave me alone.'

There's a cheer from the dance floor as a new song starts, something by the Rolling Stones. 'The old ones are the best ones,' I say.

'So they say.'

'What do you want to do now, Alice?'

She leans towards me again, her mouth inches away from mine. 'Do you want to come back to mine?'

'Are you sure?'

She nods her head. 'Well… I think so.'

I know what she means; it seems indecently hasty. But I want her so much, a longing the likes of which I've never experienced before. It's like a physical pain burying itself deep within me. 'Perhaps we should wait?'

'Yes,' she says. 'I think you're right.'

We both pick up our drinks and watch the girls on the dance floor, dancing without inhibition, dancing as if there was no tomorrow. I envy them but I wouldn't want to be any of them because, right now, there's nowhere on earth I'd rather be, and no person on this planet I'd rather be than me sitting here, sipping my drink, next to Alice while my nerve ends sizzle with desire.

'Fuck it,' says Alice, slamming her near-empty glass on the table. 'I can't bear it.' She stands up. 'I'm taking you back to mine whether you want to or not, even if I have to drag you by your tie.'

I'm not wearing a tie but I take her point. She holds out her hand. I take it. But before we move, she stands on tiptoe and kisses me. The girls on the dance floor cheer again. But this time, they're not cheering for a song, they're cheering at us kissing. Alice and I smile while, holding hands, Alice leads the way out of Celsius.

It's not far from the bar to Alice's flat but we see a taxi

cruising by and hail it. Three minutes later, we're there. She fumbles with her key, unable to coordinate herself enough to unlock the bloody door. 'Come on, come on,' she says to herself. Finally, she gets it right and we're in.

The flat is warm and welcoming. She slams the door shut behind me. I turn to face her. We look at each other under the glare of the hallway light bulb. Her eyes flare and I know she wants me. A surge of electricity passes between us. A moment of hesitation. And then we kiss with a violence that takes us both by surprise.

Our lips barely part as we stagger from the hallway to the bedroom. We stand against the bed. Quickly, she unbuttons my shirt, and yanks it off. I remove my tee-shirt underneath. 'I love your tattoos, Mac.' She runs her finger down the lion head that dominates the left side of my chest. My skin tingles at her touch. Then, looking up at me again, she kisses me.

My cock is truly hard now in my trousers, it's aching. I'm desperate to free him but I don't want to rush it. Somehow, being in Alice's flat, I feel she should dictate how fast we move this. We're still kissing as I fumble with the first daisy-shaped button on her yellow blouse. I manage to undo them all, she flings her shirt off and I gape at her pale-yellow bra holding up her pert, wonderful breasts. My heartbeat speeds up, my cock, already so hard, hardens further.

She pulls my jeans down. I step out of them, a little less gainly than I would've liked, but we're in such a hurry now. She whips off her bra, throwing it aside and my heart hammers on seeing her naked breasts and the size of her nipples. She cups her tits, a smile playing on her lips. 'I want you to suck me,' she says through gritted teeth.

I dive on it like a man starved. I flick my tongue around the nipple gently first, most gently.

We fall onto the bed. I lie on top of her and we kiss, hesitantly at first, like two strangers getting to know each other. But it doesn't take long for the sap to rise, for the desire to burn. She buries her fingers into my arse, her nails hard and sharp, almost breaking the skin. She yanks her skirt down and then opens her legs, and I can see how wet she is by the dampness of her yellow knickers. I salivate just at the sight of her. She lets out a cry as I suck at her pussy through her panties, making the wet fabric wetter still. She pulls on my hair, yelping, a sound that turns me on no end and makes me frenzied. My tongue laps up her juices. She uses a finger to hook her sodden knickers to one side, giving me full access to that delicious wet, inviting cunt, shaved and exposed and all for me. I don't need a second invitation – I bury my head into her, while using my hands to push her thighs wider and wider still. I circle her clitoris with my tongue while she whimpers, her hand scrunching my hair. She gasps and her hold on me tightens as I insert a finger into her. Her odour fills my nostrils, all woman, and it triggers a spasm within me as my balls tighten and the lust overwhelms me. The walls of her pussy clench my fingers. I run my tongue from her clit down to her hole, her wetness coating my lips, then back up. Her body trembles as I circle my tongue around that little button of pleasure. I feel her wetness in my mouth and I know she's close to climaxing here. Her body shakes, her eyes glaze over as the waves of pleasure wash over her. She whimpers and cries out my name. Her body bucks as she slaps the bed several times and grinds her cunt further into my face. I know I've never experienced a pussy so wet and so gorgeous as this.

I sit up on my knees and pull down my boxers. She lifts her head and watches as my cock springs into life. I thrust my hips forward a little, accentuating the size of me, the pure hardness of my penis. I use her wetness on my fingers to coat the entire length. I grip myself at the base. She gulps and then smiles. She runs her fingers up and down the length of my shaft, then cups my balls. She sits up, mouth open as a dew-drop of cum drips from the end of my dick. She catches it on the end of her fingertips, then sucks on her fingers. My legs give way on seeing her doing that.

She opens her legs. I crawl up the bed. I reach up and kiss her hard, frenzied even, my prick resting at her entrance. 'Are you sure?' I ask.

'Fuck, yes. Just do it, I'm desperate for this.'

'I don't have a condom.'

'Shit, yes. The drawers there, bottom drawer.'

I scramble across while she urges me to be quick. I do the business with the condom while she lies on her back in front of me playing with her clit, rubbing her finger around in little circles and mewling.

Ready now, I lie on top of her and guide my cock back to the entrance of her pussy. I rub its head up and down her, making her even more wet. I grunt as my cock slips effortlessly into her, no friction, just a glorious wet plunge. She throws her head back, squealing 'yes' over and again. Each slow stroke causes me to grind deeper inside her.

Normally, I'd build up the pace but I know how desperate she is, how desperate I am, that this is not the time for niceties so straight away I thrust hard. I pump her while watching her, our faces just an inch or two away from each other, our eyes boring into each other's. Her boobs ripple up and down with my pumping. I feel the walls of her pussy clenching tightly around me as if she's squeezing the cum from within me. She locks her legs around me, pinning me in place, making sure my throbbing cock doesn't escape her. I build up the intensity, grinding harder inside her, making her yelp for me.

'Am I tight enough for you, Mac?' she asks.

'Fuck, yeah. You're gorgeous, Alice, you know that?'

'And I'm all yours now, Mac. All yours, baby.'

I thrust harder, faster, deeper, grunting, my balls slapping against her asshole. She bucks beneath me and I know she's about to cum again.

'Yes, fuck, yes, Mac. Do it faster, harder, please, Mac, please.'

The sweat seeps down my back. I pump harder up to the point I know she's coming and then ease back a little as she arches her back, her eyes squeezed shut, and lets out a cry of such painful, earthly intensity. I slow down, allowing her to catch her breath. Her face shines red. I feel her relax beneath me. She smiles.

'Go on,' she whispers. 'Please cum, Mac. I want to feel you cum inside me. Go on,' she mutters like an injured animal. I gaze into her eyes as delicious waves of spunk explode from within me. And finally when I think there's nothing more to give, I collapse on top of her.

We lie on her bed, our chests heaving. I laugh gently. She turns towards me and droops her arm across my chest. 'Well, Mac, what can I say?'

We catch our breaths, our heartbeats slowly edging down and returning to normal. After a while, we both feel the need to cover ourselves. I admire her bedroom which I'd seen the other day from the landing. It has maroon walls, and a large, Ikea-style wardrobe and a rather old-fashioned-looking dresser with a large oval mirror, slightly decorated. The room is wall-to-wall carpeted with a pale violet carpet. The whole room is infused with warmth and love, and you can see Alice in every bit of it. It is, without doubt, Alice's room.

'You OK?' I ask her.

She pats my hand. 'Yeah. You?'

'Yeah.'

'Would you like to stay the night?'

'Would that be OK?'

She smiles. 'Sure. I was hoping you'd say that.'

Chapter 10: Mac

Today, the sun is out, the shop is loud and busy, we've got The Killers playing on the stereo, the till is constantly pinging and I feel on top of the world. It's been a long, long time since I've felt like this, if indeed I have *ever* felt like this, and it's all down to one single human being. Is this how people actually feel when they are happy, as in truly happy? I want to ask Tony and Eoin but I fear I'd come across as either a bit sad or a bit strange or probably both.

Alice and I woke up together. We would have had more sex but time was against us. It is, after all, a normal working day today and we both had places to be. So after quick showers (separate, mind you, because we didn't trust each other not to get carried away if we showered together), she made me a very large and hearty breakfast, for which I was very thankful. I'd forgotten how much of appetite sex can give a person. It was so lovely sitting in her flat, eating breakfast in her kitchen, drinking strong coffee and listening to the radio. I admired Van Gogh's Sunflowers. We left her flat together, saying goodbye to the ginger cat, and walked to our respective places of work, holding hands. It felt like the happiest morning of my life. My shop was the first one on the route. We stopped a fair distance away from the shop in case either Tony or Eoin appeared. We kissed again, not wanting it to end. I watched her walk away from me, and as she reached her turning, she stopped and waved at me. She knew I'd be watching.

It was only as I was unlocking the shop and deactivating the alarm that I thought of my father and my mood punctured.

My mind and my whole being had been so wrapped up in Alice that I'd not given Dad a thought so that when, finally, I did, I experienced a horrible rush of guilt. The man was poorly, how poorly no one seemed to know. I rang the care home before we opened and spoke to Mrs Hale, the manager.

'No improvement, I'm afraid, Mr MacIntosh.'

'Has he eaten anything?'

'No. We tried to tempt him with a little bit of hot chicken soup but he wasn't interested, he just refused point blank to eat a thing. I'm sorry.' She sounds tired, poor woman.

'It's not your fault. What do we do next though?'

'If there's no improvement by the end of today, we'll make an appointment for the doctor to come see him tomorrow morning. I'll let you know if there's any developments, Mr MacIntosh.'

I thanked her.

That was first thing. So now, it's mid-morning and we're busy, the shop is buzzing and I'm happy again. Today is the day we offer pensioners a big discount on their haircuts. It was my dad's idea a while back, when he was still in control of his mind, and it took a while to take off but slowly the word got round to the point Wednesday is now our busier day of the week after Saturday. So, as per usual on a Wednesday, we had lots of older guys in, making the most of the offer. Alicia Keys is playing on the stereo. I always enjoy it; it's good to speak to the old guys, they're always so interesting. The only downside is that it brings it home just how far my father's mind has deteriorated. He used to be an interesting guy, albeit a resentful and bitter one at times, but no one could blame him for that, not after what he'd been through.

I've just finished cutting an old guy's hair. He spent the whole time here talking about a driving trip he and his mate did through Italy back in the seventies. In this job, you hear a lot of stuff and much of it, it has to be said, can be a tad dull, but you learn to 'oo' and 'er' a lot and smile and laugh in the right places. But to be fair, this guy could have been the most interesting and funniest man in the world and I would have had a hard time concentrating when all I can think about is Alice's breasts and the way she screamed when I came inside her. The woman consumes my every waking moment. I literally can't get her out of my mind. And it is lovely. I've never felt like this before, didn't think I was capable of it. It's a feeling that, I realise, leaves you feeling warm inside.

My old guy left me a generous tip, twenty per cent or more. He can come back any time! It's as he's leaving and I'm thinking about coffee that I hear the ding-dong notification on my mobile.

I tell the next guy I'll be with him in just a moment. Having a few moments to myself, I look at my phone and open up my email, wondering whether this could be from the mysterious woman Eoin mentioned yesterday afternoon. There is a new email with the subject heading, Hello. My nerves are on edge as I open the email up while Taylor Swift plays loudly, too loudly, on the stereo.

Dear Thomas.

Thomas? Only people who don't know me call me Thomas.

Dear Thomas,
I know this may come as a bit of a shock but I am your mother.

Oh fuck. *Fuck.* I slam the phone back in my back pocket. I feel dizzy, I need to sit down. The music's too loud, my head is pounding all of a sudden. Tony, who's with a customer, notices. 'Jesus, Mac, you all right? You look ill, mate.'

'Yeah, I'm not…' I'm fighting for breath here, this is mad. 'I just need some air. It's too hot in here.'

'Sure.'

I apologise to my next customer, telling him I'd be back in a minute.

It's warm outside, the sky fairly clear. I walk towards the post office where I know there's a couple of benches. One of them is vacant. I sit down, my legs feeling like jelly. I don't want to read this email but I know I will. It's there, on my phone, waiting for me, a message from my mother. It doesn't seem true. I never thought this day would come. I look up and catch the eye of a young mum passing by, holding the hand of a small boy of about four or five. It sees like an omen. I hold my breath as I start to read.

I hope you're OK, son. I think of you every day. I managed to find your email address with the help of a friend. I live in Spain now but since Brexit it's more difficult living here now as a Brit. So I'm coming to London to check on a few flats I've seen online. Thomas, I know you may not want to see me, but I would love to see you again. I know it'll be hard for you but please come see me. I know you probably still hate me for running out of your life like I did but please believe me — if I could change things I'd do so in a heartbeat.
I still love you.

Mum.

I can't control my heart; it's thumping so hard. I want to be sick. I stare up to the sky and then clench my eyes shut. I can't believe I've just read what I've read. She's been in Spain all this time. And now she's back and she wants to see me. She finishes her email with her mobile number and the hotel where she's staying in London.

There were times when I'd have given anything, *anything*, to receive this email. But now? After all this time? No, it's too late now. I'm not interested. I'm not going to jump at the sound of my mother clicking her fingers at me. No, not now. I look at the email again, this time more slowly, but it makes no difference. This woman ruined my life, and I'm not letting her back in to ruin it again. No way.

I delete the email.

Chapter 11: Mac

There's so much from my childhood I don't remember. I recall
snatches here and there but there's these long lapses where I
have only a vague sense of what was happening in my life, like
the vaguest of Impressionist paintings. I remember my mother
as a very loving and warm person but of course that memory
of her is totally sullied by the fact that she saw fit to walk out
on her husband and her nine-year-old child, never to return.
What sort of woman does that? What drove her away? Or,
more likely, what drew her away? That was always Dad's
theory, that Mum went to live with another man somewhere.
He was right, had to be, because it was, and still is, the only
logical explanation. Her name was Iris, a good, old-fashioned
name. I was at that age when I no longer wanted to be cuddled
by her because I was too big now. But boy, once she'd gone,
I'd have given anything for one of her hugs. I remember she
always wore a lot of make-up. Bright red lipstick and stuff
around her eyes. I didn't like it. Yes, it made her look pretty
but I didn't want pretty, I just wanted Mum. I remember she
was also very clumsy. Whenever I drop anything or trip over

something, I think, *just like Mum.*

I can't believe that after all this time, she's contacted me. I'd already been thinking more about her after I'd met Alice but now it was obsessing me. I'd deleted the email, having no desire to see her again. Why should I allow her this chance of redemption when she'd forced me into a childhood of misery? I don't want to see this older version of my mother begging me for my forgiveness. It's too late now, woman. I don't need you now, where were you when I did need you, when Dad and I needed you? But despite deleting her email, despite promising myself I want nothing to do with her, I can't stop thinking about her. And frankly, it's annoying because her email has come just at the point I thought I might have something with Alice and there's my mother to remind me that I'm fated when it comes to women. Every girlfriend I've had it's ended in tears because I know what I'm like: I'm terrified they'll run off one day, that they'll get bored of me sooner or later and go off to pastures new. I cannot, must not, allow that to happen again, I cannot afford to be emotionally ripped apart like that ever again. I can't allow Alice to do it to me. I can't allow her to get too close.

I used to stay at my grandparents' house twice a week. They lived only a ten-minute drive away but I hated it after a while, they never seemed particularly pleased to see me, and I could never understand why I needed to sleep there so often. But every week, school or no school, Mum drove me there before tea and dropped me off. She never stayed to speak to them. They were Dad's parents and I don't think my grandparents and Mum ever really got on, looking back on it They'd give me my tea which I ate in front of the TV and then I'd watch TV for the rest of the evening – until the time I had to go to bed, which was always, to my young mind, far too early. Then, the next day, Granny or Grandpa would drop me off either at school or at home. If at home, Mum would greet me with a big hug and a kiss. And then the day came that will always be imprinted in my mind, the day I knew that love was worthless; the day my mother left and never came back. I returned home from school and opened the front door with my key. I knew straight away that something felt off, that the house was too quiet. I called for my mum and received no reply. And that's when I saw the little white card propped up against the kettle with my name on it: Thomas. I flipped it over and the words pierced me leaving me gasping for air:

My dearest Thomas, I'm so sorry. One day I hope you will forgive me, Mum.

That was it. But it was enough – I knew she'd gone. I rang her mobile and got an automated message saying this number had been removed or some such message. I didn't know what to do – did Dad know, Grandpa or Granny? I rang Dad, wondering what I'd say if he didn't, I mean, how do you break something like this to someone. The call went through to his voicemail and I couldn't leave a message; it was too important for that. I tried again, about three or four times and never got through, so I knew I just had to wait for him to return from work. I always knew I didn't want to show him Mum's note to me, I knew Mum meant it for me and me only. So I hid it in one of my books, I even remember the book to this day – it was one of the Harry Potters. Dad came in about half past six, his usual time, by which time I was starving. 'Where's Mum?' was the first thing he asked. 'What's for dinner?'

I shook my head. 'I don't know where Mum is, she wasn't here when I got back.'

That stopped Dad in his tracks. He looked at me weirdly as if what I was saying didn't make sense. And then he ran from room to room shouting her name, 'Iris, Iris, Iris?' He pounded upstairs and I could hear each door opening and slamming shut. Then, he returned downstairs and then repeated the whole circuit again, even going outside to check in the garden shed, as if she was hiding in there. He finally stopped and he looked grey and exhausted.

He slammed his fist onto the dining room table. 'The bitch,' he yelled. 'The bloody bitch.'

I knew Mum had done wrong by running off but I still didn't like it when he used that word. 'Where is she, Dad?'

He shook his head, the sweat pouring off him, catching his breath. 'I don't know, son. I don't bloody know.' He wiped his brow and blew his nose and then he said something else, something that haunted me: 'All I know is if I ever catch her…' He didn't finish the sentence, just left it hanging there, and for years I wondered about those unsaid words. We looked at each other and I willed myself to hold his gaze. I so wanted to tell him I was hungry. More than hungry, I felt weak with hunger. Then, without a word, Dad scooped up his coat he'd thrown on the back of a dining room chair and, checking his pockets for his phone and keys, went out, slamming the front door behind him.

I stood there, wondering what to do, how to feed myself, who to ask for help. And I realised there was no one, just… no one at all. And that's when I collapsed on the armchair and sobbed.

.

Chapter 12: Mac

I take Alice to the White Oak tonight. I introduce her to Eoin and Tony. As always, the music is loud, the customers already drunk and the atmosphere buzzing. The boys are delighted to see Alice, falling over themselves to talk to her, not that they were hitting on her, they wouldn't dare, but they want to welcome her to the fold, our gang, sometimes called the White Oak Gang sometimes Mac's Gang. They jostle her a little, tease her about her height and challenging her to a game of darts. Eoin even challenges her to a drinking contest. Tony hits him. 'That's unfair, you twerp,' he says loudly. 'Your belly naturally holds more beer than a beer barrel.'

Eoin presses his belly in as if he needed reminding just how big it is. After all, the man's about six foot six, Tony too. I'm not far behind, but I'm the relative short arse at six foot three. Jack is an inch taller than me. No one messes with blokes our size. They were playing around for her, preening themselves like a pair of peacocks. I told myself not to get jealous of all this, and given what I had planned, I had absolutely no right to. It's Eoin who catches my eye and he knows straight away that I'm not happy with all this banter over Alice. 'Anyhow, Alice,' he says. 'Let's all sit down and have a quiet drink.'

'Quiet?' she says. 'In this place?'

'We can but try,' says Tony, pulling a seat out for her like an old-fashioned gentleman.

Eoin comes up to me. 'So, how's it going, the two of you?' he asks.

'Yeah, good.'

He looks at me askance, perhaps surprised, even disappointed, by the lacklustre reply. But what could I tell him, that I am already thinking of ending it with Alice before it had even begun because I was hung up on the thought of her leaving me? Luckily, our attention is caught by Tony's booming voice.

'So how's it going with Jack then?' he asks Alice. 'Is he settling in, the traitor?'

'You'll be able to ask him yourself in a while. He's popping in with Ian and his mates.'

'Is he?' cries Eoin. 'He's not sitting with us; I'll tell you that for nothing.'

'I thought you were friends?'

'We were,' I say, trying to shut the conversation down.

'We're rivals,' says Eoin. 'Top Cutz and us. Business rivals, creative rivals, the lot.'

'Yeah,' says Tony. 'So you don't jump teams just because the other offers you a penny an hour more, we're worth more than that, and he knows it.'

'But people move on all the time.'

'Sure,' I say. 'That's fine. We've no problem with that. But go to a barber out of town or to a different business, anything but–'

'Go to our direct competitors,' finishes Eoin for me.

'So have you always wanted to cut hair?' asks Tony.

Alice laughs. 'Am I being interviewed again?'

'No but really? Unless you get in with a cool crowd like us, it's not always the most glamorous of occupations.'

'That's why I wanted to get in with a cool gang like yours.' She throws me a look that cuts me short.

'Men's hair though?' asks Tony.

'Men are easier: easier to please and easier to impress.'

'Yes, well...' says Eoin. 'That's true, I guess.'

'Hair is important for all of us, but for women especially, it's vital to get it right, it's all about confidence and feeling good about yourself.'

I stand up and somehow manage to walk straight into a chair.

Tony and Eoin laughed. 'Clumsy,' says Tony.

I shake my head. 'For God's sake, I take after my mother.'

'Your mother?' asks Eoin.

'She was clumsy, always accident-prone and bumping into things.'

I go to the bar to get a round of drinks while the boys and Alice talk shop. I watch the three of them together from the bar, talking, laughing, as if they'd known each other for years, and my head is full of if onlys... if only I'd taken her on in the first place and not become her lover. We could have been together, the four of us, the best of mates. Instead, I'd been stupid and allowed her to fall into Ian's clutches.

Many songs and a few pints later, Tony, Eoin and Alice are dancing to some shit dance track when Ian, Jack and the Top Cutz boys make their entrance. I half watch them as they circle around the place, making sure that everyone knows that they have arrived. Alice, on seeing them, comes and stands next to me. We are the last to receive the royal visit. 'Hey, Alice,' shouts Ian above the music. 'What are you doing, girl? You're one of us now.'

Alice throws me a glance, unsure whether to spill the beans about her and me.

This, I decide, is as good a time as any. 'Ian s right, you know, Alice. You can't be in both places at once, can you? Not in our turf war. It's not right. I reckon you need to make a choice. What side do you play for? You can't have one foot in one camp and the other in the other camp.'

'You what?' she gasps. 'Are you...?' She looks confused, as well as she might be. I want to apologise, to take it back, but I think of my father and I know I can't back off now; I've come this far. I'm hating myself right now but I know I'll thank myself in the long run.

She sidles up to me and I can see the anger and the hurt in her eyes. 'You know I need this job, Mac. I can't just give it up.'

'It's your choice, Alice. Ian's job or me.'

She can't believe what's she's hearing although, frankly, nor can I. 'You are fucking joking with me, Mac. This is your idea of a sick joke, isn't it?'

I don't move, I don't say a word. Ian's holding his ground, enjoying the spectacle.

And then it fully registers. 'Oh my god,' she breathes. 'You're being fucking serious. I don't believe it. You bastard, Mac. You utter, utter bastard.'

And that was the point I simply had to walk away.

Chapter 13: Mac

I remember Dad used to take me to the betting shop occasionally. Back then, people could still smoke indoors and these places always stunk of smoke, the ceilings were yellow and the carpet pockmarked with countless cigarette burns. Dad would pick me up after school and we went straight there even though I protested that I was hungry and couldn't we go home first. I remember the first time. Dad wanted to bet on a particular horse in a particular race. The odds were good and Dad was feeling confident. The race started and Dad was on his feet, hopping from one foot to the other, watching the race on one of those large, overhead TV screens. I knew that despite his bravado, now that the race had started, he was worried about this, that winning this bet was important. I didn't see how much money he gave the woman behind the cashier desk but I reckoned it was a lot, more than he should be gambling. That's when I knew that the outcome of this race would have a direct bearing on my immediate future too. The horse was called Arpeggio, his jockey wore purple with a large diagonal orange stripe. My heart sank to see him in almost last place. Dad started shouting at the TV. I was on my feet too, my heart in my mouth. I felt sick. He had to win, just had to. There were other men who'd bet on other horses in the race and the noise got louder and louder and the tension palpable. I willed Arpeggio on. He seemed to be catching up. There were only a few fences to jump but one horse in particular, Genie in a Bottle, was a long way ahead. Arpeggio was now in second place, doing well and far ahead of the horse in third place but with one fence to go he was too far behind. Dad was pulling his hair out. And then – a miracle: Genie in a Bottle fell at the last fence. All Arpeggio had to do was clear that last fence… Dad and I held our breaths, our eyes out on stalks, glued to that TV screen. And he did it! He was over, and way ahead of all the other horses. He trotted home in first place and Dad and I jumped in the air and screamed with joy. Dad collected his money from the cashier who laughed at what she called his beginner's luck, and we left the bookmakers on cloud nine. He took me to our local McDonald's and told me I could have anything I wanted. We ate like kings that night, and for the first time since Mum had left, I went to bed happy.

Of course, what I didn't appreciate at the time was that it was nothing but a false victory, a Pyrrhic victory, and that it would have been so much better in the long run had Dad lost that bet. Because, like the cashier said, it was beginner's luck, winning with his first bet. It gave Dad a taste of what it was like to win easy money. I didn't realise at the time but Dad went back to that same bookmaker again and again hoping to recapture the euphoria of that first win, and occasionally he did, but it was rare. Mostly, he lost and lost badly. Soon, he'd lost everything he'd won with Arpeggio and more, much more. And life at home became harder. We never had any heating on at home. If I complained, he'd just tell me to put another jumper on. Getting up for school in the mornings was horrible because the house was so awfully cold. And yet every week Dad still went off to the bookmakers with his social security money and lost it all. He'd come back in a foul temper and took it out on me. Once, when I dared ask if we could go back to McDonald's, I thought he was going to hit me, he was so angry. I never asked again and we never went again.

*

Alice and I had arranged to go to the care home together but after our parting the night before, I wasn't looking forward to picking her up. Nonetheless, after work, I show up at hers with the car. The sun is still warm, this patch of North London still bathed in sunshine. But I wasn't feeling it inside. I press on her buzzer, expecting her to say she'd be down shortly. Instead, she asks me to come up. So I do.

I brace myself for a confrontation, saying hello to the ginger cat that seems to live on the communal stairs as a means of calming myself, but I was worrying unnecessarily. Alice welcomes me with a hug and a kiss. She looks fantastic in her ever-so tight dark blue jeans and a white blouse tied into a bow at the bottom. But I feel I still need to address this particular elephant in the room. 'Look, Alice, I'm sorry I was such an arse last night.'

'It's fine, Mac. But…'

'Yes?'

'What's the matter, Mac? I can sense something about you, an unease of some sort. Sometimes I look at you and you look worried about things, as if you're frightened your shadow might creep up on you and bite you.'

I laugh, albeit a forced one, and say, 'Well, that just about sums it up.'

She gazes out of the window for a while. 'I'm not asking you, Mac, I'm not gonna press you but anytime you want to talk about it, I'll be here. Whatever it is, Mac, I'll listen and I promise, I won't judge you.'

'Thank you.'

'Come here,' she says, beckoning me with a crooked finger as if pulling me in by an invisible thread. I'm happy to be hauled in. She puts her arms around me and kisses me, gently at first, but with greater intensity with every passing second. I don't want to react but I can't prevent my cock from stirring in my trousers. 'Have we time?' she asks.

'No,' I say, hoping she'll contradict me.

'Fuck that, we do.'

'No, Alice, listen…'

She unties that bow on her blouse and whips it off. 'We can be quick,' she whispers, removing her bra and allowing her wonderful breasts to fall free. And that's it, resistance shattered, mind blown, cock rock hard. I hardly have time to process this rapid turn of events when she removes her jeans. 'Come,' she barks, her eyes narrowed. 'Bed now.'

She throws off her panties and throws herself on the bed. 'I'm not asking you, Mac, I'm telling you – I want you inside me now. I'm dripping for you.' Her beauty stuns me for a moment.

She spreads her legs for me, revealing the vivid redness of her wet gash. My heart somersaults at the sight of it, that delicious pussy all for me. I dive in, my tongue working up and down her clit. 'Your fingers, Mac. Put your fingers in.'

I delay a moment, circling my finger around her pussy, my knuckle brushing her labia. Her breathing intensifies. She spreads her legs wider still, leaving her entirely exposed to me. Sweat trickles down my back. I insert one finger inside her. I soon realise she's so wet she'd hardly feel it, so I insert two fingers. She cries out as her body arches up, her fingers scrunching the duvet. My fingers pump in time with the up and down movement of my mouth. Her hips start to gyrate in time. I take my finger out and drag a path of her wetness down the inside of her thigh.

I flick my tongue again around her clitoris. Christ, she tastes sweet and so smooth, smooth as silk. I suck her labia into my mouth, chewing on those wonderful little nodules of flesh. My cock leaks droplets of cum. She pushes herself against me, pushing her cunt harder against my mouth. Her fingers yank at my hair while ramming me even further into the abyss of her vagina. She begins muttering, 'I'm coming, Mac, oh my god, how did you do that so fast? I'm coming, I'm coming!'

She shakes and quivers, and mewls loudly, her eyes clenched shut, before slowly, very slowly, she comes down. She pants and giggles a little.

She thinks we've finished, but we have not, oh no, woman. 'My turn now,' I say. 'I want you on all fours right now.'

She does as told, and, on her hands and knees, thrusts her ass out, exposing her cunt to me. I take my raging cock and inch towards her, and gently rub my bulging red helmet up and down her wetness. She gasps. She drops her head and her hair cascades down. I place my knob right at her entrance, pushing in just ever so slightly. She cries out for more. I give her another inch, no more. I watch the white fluid of her cream pool around my shaft. She tenses up. Then, with a mighty thrust, I plunge into her, making her cry out in half ecstasy, half pain. God, she's deliciously tight. I grip her hips, and thrust harder and harder, increasing the intensity, making her yelp. I love the way her pussy stretches around my cock. It feels perfect. Her boobs jiggle with each thrust and the sight of that is like a live wire to my balls. I can feel the sap rising within me and I know it won't be long now. 'I'm gonna erupt, Alice.'

'Not like this,' she cries. 'I want to see your face as you come. Please, Mac.'

I remove my cock from inside her. She twists around and lies on her back and opens her legs. Her slit glistens and I think I'm going to come right there over her. I manage to plunge my dick back inside her. We kiss as I fuck her, her fingers weaving through my hair.

My balls tighten as the cum rises up within me, I can feel it traversing the length of my shaft as I hump her frantically, desperate to come and desperate to keep going for as long as possible. I groan loudly. A couple more deep, deep thrusts and I'm almost there. Sure enough, seconds later, my hips buck as I come, my cock shuddering deep, deep inside her. She screams my name as she pushes back and grinds on my spurting cock. Oh. My. God. I drain every last drop into her, giving her all of me until I have nothing left to give. I am spent.

I slip out of her and, my back to her, discreetly remove the condom. We fall on her bed, our chests still heaving, both grinning like the proverbial Cheshire cat. We are happy, deliciously happy. If only time had stopped here.

Chapter 14: Mac

We drive to the care home in silence, a smile on our lips. Sex alone cannot cure the world but boy, it comes close sometimes. Our bodies still feel warm, both inside and out, glowing and caressed, our hearts likewise. It's such a rarity, this feeling, and I can see why people are addicted to it. This, I think, must be what love feels like. I glance at the woman in the passenger seat beside me and try to remember how this came about, why this wondrous, beautiful woman should lay herself so open for me, both physically and emotionally. I feel honoured in a strange, old-fashioned way, and certainly lucky. I smile to myself as I take a left turn.

'A penny for your thoughts,' she says.

'Oh!' I laugh. 'I was just thinking what a lucky guy I am.'

She winks at me. 'You sure are.' She bites on her fingernail, then: 'And I am too, one lucky gal to have found a bear like you.'

I growl at her and I know I could live in this moment forever.

'Mac, would you like to meet my grandmother?'

'Sure. Although actually, I've spoken to her many times over the last couple of years. She often wanders around with a cup and saucer in her hand.'

Alice laughs. 'Yes, spilling tea everywhere. She likes to keep an eye on everyone. I think it comes from being a headmistress for years.'

'She's always neatly dressed.'

'Oh yes, that sort of thing is important, isn't it? However old you are, you want to look your best. It's all about dignity, don't you think?'

'Yeah.' I think of Dad and I don't remember much dignity there.

'Can I meet your father?' she asks.

My heart hardens, my fingers grip the steering wheel. I try to keep my voice even as I answer. 'Oh? Yeah, erm, sure, I mean if you really want to.' I wasn't expecting this and I don't like the idea of it at all. But how can I say no without causing offence? 'I'm mean, he doesn't usually say much so you won't get much out of him and–'

'That's fine, I'm not expecting to. I just thought… I don't know, that it'd be nice to meet your father. Who knows he might tell me something about you.'

'I doubt it.' She throws me a glance, catching my dismissive tone.

'There's no need to look so worried, Mac.'

'I'm sorry. It's just that… Dad's not the easiest of people, I mean even before he fell ill, he was tough to live with. You see…'

We arrive at Sunny Grove care home and I park in the suburban street nearby. 'Here we are,' I say unnecessarily, and I realise I'm worried about this. I can't remember the last time Dad met someone I knew, a friend. He's certainly never met a girlfriend of mine.

Alice places her hand on my knee. 'Go on. You were about to say.'

I take a deep breath, and I tell her. I tell her that my mother left Dad and I totally out of the blue. I certainly hadn't been expecting it and I don't think Dad had either. And that the experience changed us for the worse – both of us. I had the resilience of youth on my side, and I had school and my friends and I went to a youth club. Dad had nothing; Mum had left him high and dry, with a lad to look after, and all he had was some crappy job that paid so much less than he needed to keep a roof over our heads. I didn't tell her about the gambling, his foul temper, the language he often used against me. Dad had it tough, he was embittered, naturally, and probably frightened. He took it out on me. I sort of understood that now, but it took a while. I'm sure Alice wouldn't understand, so I kept that bit away from her, she didn't need to know. I don't know how long I talk for but after a while I come to a halt. I stare out of the window watching a mother in the near distance pushing a toddler on a three-wheeler bicycle.

'Hell,' says Alice eventually. 'What a story, your poor dad, poor you. How awful.'

'Yeah, well, like I say it was tougher on Dad really. I sort of got used to it after a while but he never did. He never got over it.'

'And you never heard from her again.'

'No,' I say firmly, thinking about the email I received just the day before yesterday now deleted and already forgotten about.

'How weird. What sort of woman deserts her child like that, and never to seek them out again? It's so wrong, isn't it?'

'Yeah.'

She runs a finger down the side of my face. It's a nice gesture. 'I can see why your father means so much to you now.'

'Shall we go?'

We put on our face masks. 'Yes, let's go.'

The care home usually smells slightly unpleasant of school dinner-type food. Today is no different. Alice pulls a face at me and we suppress a giggle. We sign in and say hello to a couple of carers. She sees her grandmother in the conservatory, the famous Mrs Charlton. 'Come back and say hello whenever you're free.' I watch her kiss her grandmother hello.

I find my father in his usual place gazing out over the garden. Another guy is talking to him, a much younger man, probably in his early fifties, in a wheelchair, and for a moment I think it might be a visitor but no, I recognise him – another patient. Gee, dementia at such a young age. Life can be shit sometimes. Dad's not listening to him but the younger guy hasn't cottoned on yet. On seeing me, the chap waves hello and then wheels himself off.

'Hi, Dad. How's it going?'

He turns and looks at me and I wait, hoping for some form of recognition, and it does come, it just takes a long while. He talks about the robin outside again and about the bird table 'back at home'. Of course, he's referring to his childhood home, not my home. Then he mentions his father again: 'He has a temper on him, my dad. Best keep out of his way.' I get this nasty feeling Dad spent much of his childhood cowering in his garden, watching the birds and looking for hedgehogs and digging up worms and kicking a football about, anything to avoid going back indoors and confronting his dad. He's unusually chatty today so I sit back and let him talk. We have our usual conversation about what he had for lunch. It always sounds wondrous! Such a shame it's always fictional. Then, he asks, 'How's that bird of yours? Alice? Was that her name?'

I'm astonished – he remembers the conversation we had the other day and he remembers her name? I'm so delighted by this lucid moment I almost want to hug him but no, we were never tactile with each other and I know it would only alarm and possibly upset him, so I keep my place, sitting on my hands. 'Yeah, well, Dad, funny you should ask about Alice because…'

'You're an item, the two of you?'

'Yeah, we are and you'll never guess but she's Mrs Charlton's daughter. You know, the woman who comes round with her cup of tea and checks up on you and asks whether you've eaten.'

'Oh, God, her? She's that nosey parker's daughter, is she? Well, good luck with that one.'

'Would you like to meet her? Alice, I mean.'

'Meet her? Me? No.'

'Oh right. It's just that Alice is here right now, visiting her grandmother, and she'd really like to meet you, Dad. I can't say no, can I? So, I'm going to bring her over in a moment and I need you to promise me that you'll be nice to her and be on your best behaviour.'

He folds his arms and returns his attention to the garden.

'Dad? Are you listening to me?'

'I don't want to meet no one.'

I take a deep breath. 'Well, sometimes, just occasionally, we have to do things that we don't necessarily want to. I can hardly say no to her because… because that would just look rude. So let's bring Alice over, just say hello for a minute, and that's it. Just… Dad, please, just do this for me, just be nice to her, OK?'

At least his mind is relatively sharp today; in fact, quite the sharpest I've known for a long while. He'll be able to hold his own in a short conversation. He'll be polite and smile in the right places and everything will be fine!

So why is it when I go and find Alice, I'm wondering why am I doing this, why am I putting myself through it. It's only going to end in tears.

Chapter 15: Alice

Mac smiles at me as he approaches. My grandmother follows my gaze and, on seeing him, says, 'Is this the chap you were talking about?'

'Yes, Gran.'

'He's big, isn't he? Good looking man, though. What did you say he does?'

'He's a barber, Gran. Cuts hair.'

'Yes, I know what a barber is. Why doesn't he have a proper job like, I don't know, a doctor or something?'

'Well, you can ask him yourself. He *is* standing right beside you.'

She throws him a look that isn't altogether encouraging. 'You cut hair?'

'Yes.'

'You look like you should be shearing sheep or working in an abattoir.'

'Gran!'

Mac laughs. 'I think cutting hair is probably easier.'

'I dare say.' She turns to me and asks, in a quieter voice, 'So, have the two of you… you know…'

'Right!' I stand. 'I think on that note, we'll go see Mac's dad.' I bend down and kiss my grandmother and tell her I'll pop by to say goodbye before I leave.

Mac and I pause between the dining area and the conservatory. 'Sorry about that,' I say.

He kisses me. 'Don't be silly. It's fine. I know what it's like.'

'That's what they say, isn't it? About dementia, how it removes your brain's gatekeeper so you end up saying things a normal person wouldn't dare.'

'Yeah, but we still think those things.'

'How's your father?'

'Let's find out, shall we?'

'You lead the way.'

Mac's father is sitting in a chair in the conservatory, just staring out of the window, watching the birds on the bird table and the trees swaying behind. His eyes are closed

'Dad?' says Mac. 'Dad, are you awake?' He opens his eyes. 'Ah, Dad. I said I'd bring Alice, my girlfriend, to come meet you. Well…' He sweeps his arm out and I step into his view. 'This is her, this is Alice. Alice, this is my father.'

I step forward, offering my hand. But Mac's Dad doesn't take it. He looks at my hand for a few seconds as if sizing it up, as if deciding whether it's safe, but then he pointedly turns his head away and returns his attention to the garden. It doesn't matter, it's fine, but no, I can't disguise my real feelings – it *does* matter.

Mac steps forward. 'Dad, don't you want to say hello?'

No answer.

'Dad, this is Alice. Like I said, Alice is my girlfriend.' I smile at that, I'm not used to hearing the word and it still sounds so nice and fresh. I'm Mac's *girlfriend.*

His father makes a *phah* sort of sound. And, like an arrow, it goes straight to my heart.

'What did you say?' asks Mac.

I reach out for him. 'It doesn't matter, Mac.'

'No, it *does*. I said, Dad, what did you say?' I knew he was getting angry with him and that it wouldn't help but that he couldn't stop himself. 'Dad, I want you to say hello to Alice.'

The man folds his arms and the look of defiance is there to see.

Mac rubs his eyes and groans. 'Don't hide, Dad. I know what you're doing.'

This is beginning to get embarrassing. 'Please, Mac, maybe he's just tired or… or confused. My gran can be like this at times.'

Mac spins around in anger, turning his back on me. 'Why does he always do this? *Why*?' He turns back to face his father, trying, perhaps, to read his stone-hard expression. Then, he seems to deflate as if realising there was no point in staying. He holds out his hand for me. 'Let's go. I'm sorry.'

'She looks like your mother,' says a hard voice behind us.

'What?' says Mac. 'No, she doesn't. Mum was dark, for one thing.'

'Yes, but she has that same slutty look.'

I stagger back. Did he just say that?

'Take my advice, son. Tell her to fling her hook. I'm telling you, she's the same type as your mother, all smiles and nice, but she'll leave you high and dry, you mark my words, mate. They're all bitches.'

'You… you–'

I have to intervene. 'No, Mac, leave him be. Come now.' I'm trying my best not to cry here.

'She'll break you, like your mother did to me.' His face is

bright red now, his eyes hard like ice. I see the look of hatred in Mac's eyes. I forcibly pull him away.

I take him to the dining room and hug him, not far from my grandmother. 'You need to calm down, Mac. Take a deep breath, let it go, let it go.'

'I'm sorry, Alice. I'm so so sorry. I… I don't know what to say.'

'It's fine. It's fine, Mac' But I know it isn't fine, I know from his eyes that he's still in shock, and upset on how his father had hurt me.

We stand there for what feels like ages, unable to move. One of the carers passes and says hello but gets nothing in return. Eventually, I say we need to go. First, though, I go and kiss my grandmother goodbye.

Having said goodbye to Gran, I motion for Mac to follow me out. I calm down a little, the fresh air helping, but I can feel my heart still thumping. We walk to the car, get in and drive off, without a word. I sit in the passenger seat, trying not to think about what had just happened, the anger surging through me. Mac is driving too fast; he too is still angry. How dare his father call me a 'slut', what gave him the right?

A woman pushing a pram suddenly appears in front of us. I scream Mac's name. He slams on the brakes. We surge forward in our seats, then are thrown back by our seatbelts. The woman is on a pedestrian crossing, she has every right to cross the road. She'd stopped, fear having frozen her to the spot. She glares at Mac with undisguised loathing. He puts his hand up in acknowledgement, in apology.

'Jesus, Mac,' I shout. 'What the fuck are you doing? You almost ran her over.'

'Yeah, I know, Alice. I'm not stupid.'

'Well, fucking slow down then. Stop driving like a maniac.'

A car behind us beeps its horn. We need to get a move on. Mac drives more slowly, more carefully. But inside my blood is boiling. I feel so angry by everything that's just happened.

Mac drives into my road.

'Has he always been like that?' I ask.

'Like what?'

'Like… like what? Like that, like a dick?'

'No, hang on, you can't say that–'

'No? Why not? Because he's not well? Because his brain's gatekeeper's totally broken down?'

'Because he's still my father.'

'You're sticking up for him? He called me a slut, Mac. How can you defend that?'

'I'm not, it's not him, it's–'

'His illness. So, you see, you are using that as an excuse–'

'A reason, not an excuse.'

'He said I have the same slutty look as your mother. Talk about deeply insulting two people at the same time. Jeepers, Mac, have you ever considered that maybe, just maybe, your mother had a legitimate reason to walk out on your father? Is he really the innocent party here?'

'You don't know what you're talking about.'

We'd reached my house. He parks up and switches off the ignition.

We sit there in angry silence until I ask, 'You know, I reckon it'd be quite interesting to hear your mother's perspective on this.'

'Shut up! Just shut up, will ya?'

'What?'

'You don't know what you're talking about. You've only met him once and already you're talking shit.'

'He called me a slut and a bitch, in case you hadn't noticed,

Mac. That's quite good going by anyone's standard. Maybe I'm not as tough as I thought, and I'm sorry about that but boy, that hurt, being talked about like that, that bloody *hurt*.'

I open the car door, my foot on the pavement outside. I pause, my back to him. 'I don't think you appreciate how much that hurt, Mac. Just telling me to shut up and that I'm talking shit doesn't really do it for me, you know?'

'Listen, Alice—'

'No, let me finish. I don't want to see you for a while.'

'You what?'

'In fact, let's leave it here. I just… I just don't need this in my life. Knowing you've got a father like that will just do my head in. I think it's best if I step away completely '

I step out of the car. Mac leans over, trying to stop me from closing the door. 'Alice, please wait. I'm sorry, I—'

I don't want to hear another word. 'Goodbye, Ma

I shut the car door and walk briskly up to my house. I close the door behind me, falling back against it. I feel like screaming the house down.

Chapter 16: Mac

'Have you ever considered that maybe, just maybe, your mother had a legitimate reason to walk out on your father? Is he really the innocent party here?' Alice's words rang in my ears for days.

I thought I was falling in love with Alice. She was perfect, my ten out of ten, or so I thought. But that conversation in the car has left me reeling. I can't get it out of my head. For so long, I'd looked after Dad, worried about him. The day I admitted defeat and had to take him into the care home was the second worst day of my life, the worst day being of course the day my mother walked out on us. But the day I drove Dad across town and guided him into that home was a horrible experience. 'Why are we here, son? What is this place?' he kept asking. 'We're just having a look around, Dad.'

Things like this are always more difficult when you're on your own. I had no wife to help me or offer support, no brothers or sisters. No mother. Just me. And it was hard, bloody hard.

He knew I was lying but was too confused to articulate it.

When I told him there was 'nothing to worry about', that just made him worry a whole lot more. The staff at the home were great, and that helped. They made a fuss over him, like a teacher on a new kid's first day in a new school, made him feel welcomed, a little special. They knew what they were doing. Dad loved the attention of these young women; he got all flirty with them. But I still felt like a total shit when the time came for me to leave. I remember running to the car, locking the door behind me and screaming.

I want to go see Alice, tell her I'm sorry, tell her how I feel. Because, damn it, perhaps she's right. The evening is mild, a hint of a red sky over this part of north London, slowly disappearing as night draws in. I stroll over to her house, trying to think of what to say, of how to bring this round. The closer I get, the more my nerves jangle. All I know is that I can't let my father get in the way of my love for Alice. By the time I've walked down her street, it's turned dark, the streetlamps have come on.

But as I approach her house, I can see her in the distance, getting into a car. I can see a man throwing a suitcase into the car boot. I quicken my pace. It's a taxi and Alice is going somewhere. I have to stop her before it's too late. The car pulls out. I sprint up the road, calling her name. 'Alice, wait! Stop! Alice, stop! Stop!'

But it's no good. The car indicates, picks up speed and is gone. I draw to a halt, my hands on my knees as I catch my breath. Alice hadn't heard me. Or, if she did, she hadn't wanted to.

*

Next morning.

Alice's phone is switched off. I leave a couple of texts and a WhatsApp. No response. Wasn't really expecting one, if truth be told. Still, it hurts and I'm worried.

Top Cutz is still quiet when I walk in. But it has only just opened for the day, they hadn't even put their music on yet. Ian sees me straight away. 'Aye, aye,' he says loudly. 'Come here for a proper haircut, have we?'

I'm not in the mood for his banter. I look around the shop, hoping to see Alice, not expecting to. I see his other barbers including Jack who is tidying his workstation and wiping down the chair. He sees me. 'Right, Mac?'

'Yeah.' Even an outsider would pick up on the frostiness between us. Fact is, it's hard to forgive a friend that betrays you.

Ian steps forward. 'What is it you want, Mac?'

'Alice. I wanted to have a word with her.'

'Really?' He steps right up to me. 'Funny that because so would I.'

'What do you mean?'

'In that I'd also like to have a word with our friend Alice. More than that, I'd like to see her here right this minute getting her ass in gear. But no, no sign of her. Nothing.'

I'd half expected this, the way she caught that taxi last night. You don't take a packed suitcase to go see a friend for the evening. But I need to make sure.

'She didn't say anything then?'

'Nope.'

I sigh. 'Well, if you see her again, tell her—'

'To fuck off? Yes, that's exactly what I'll be doing, who does she take me for? As far as I'm concerned, she's terminated her contract here. And if she comes running asking for a reference…' He lets the sentence hang but we all know what he's about to say. And it's obvious he has no idea where she's gone. There was no point hanging around.

I nod Ian my thanks and leave.

I've only gone twenty yards up the road, when I hear footsteps behind me. 'Mac, wait up a minute.' That's Jack's voice.

As much as I resent the man, I can't help but smile on seeing his familiar happy face, although this time he doesn't look too happy.

'Listen, Mac.' He glances behind him as if he's worried in case Ian had followed.

'What's up?'

'It's about Alice.'

OK, that's got my attention.

'She texted me this morning…'

'She did?'

'Yeah. She said something had come up and she had to get away for a while.'

I take this in. 'Did she say where?' Jack shakes his head. 'How long?'

'No, sorry, mate. But…'

'But?'

'I don't know. The tone of it, you know, it… it didn't sound like she'd be popping back anytime soon.'

'How's she been, you know, working with you guys?'

He shrugs his shoulders. 'Honestly? I thought we were doing OK. I mean, not great, sometimes she's a bit quiet, too quiet, but yeah, apart from that, everything's fine. Ian's a shit, to be sure. Always making lewd comments to her. I've told him to back off but he just laughs at me. She's a beauty, that's for sure. I don't know what you got going on with her, but you can't afford to fuck it up, man.'

'Yeah. I know.'

'Wherever she is, Mac, you need to find her, mate. Make sure she's OK and make her yours.' He puts his heavy hand on my shoulder. 'You know that, don't you?'

'Yeah.' I nod. 'Yeah, I know. Thanks, Jack.'

I watch Jack run back to Top Cutz. The air feels heavy around me. What Jack says is right – I need to find her but where? Where in the hell can she be? It's happening all over again. First my mother, now Alice. I see a poster with Taylor Swift, advertising her latest album. It was the same song on the stereo when I opened that email from my mother. I can visualise the video for the song. I know though that whenever I hear that song it won't be the video that comes to mind but the memory of me reading those words written by my mother. *If I could change things I'd do so in a heartbeat. I still love you.* Jesus.

I take my phone and open up my email app. I scroll down the deleted messages, finding the one from Mum. I'm doing this and I'm doing it now. I know if I hesitate, if I think about it for a single second, I'll back out. I find her email, the name of the hotel she's staying at near the bottom, and below it, her mobile number. I press it and let it ring, my heart hammering inside my chest to the point of causing me physical pain. And then someone answers.

'Hello? Iris Roberts here. Who's that, please?'

'Hello, Mum. It's your son here.'

Chapter 17: Mac

Bertie's Café on the Holloway Road is half-full when I get there at eleven. I am early, purposefully. I need time to prepare myself, get used to my surroundings. I step in and breathe in the delicious aromas of coffee and cinnamon. I've been to Bertie's before. George, the camp, high-pitched barista with a ponytail greets me like a long-lost friend. The place isn't too dissimilar to Mac the Clipper in terms of its feel: brick walls, wooden floor, low-hanging lampshades, movie posters and framed prints of moody Parisian street scenes. I am worried in case the music is too loud, but it's pleasant: a laid-back jazzy number. I take a seat and wait. I know this is going to be tough – I am too early. My mouth is dry, my palms damp with sweat. I can't stop my leg from jigging up and down. Every time the door opens, my heart does a somersault. I know instinctively that I will recognise her, of that I am sure. She was my mother after all, my own flesh and blood, *and she still is*. Yes, I hadn't seen her for twenty years but I'd know her anywhere.

What would we talk about? Where does one start after so long? I would have to tell her about Dad, how the dementia crept up on him at such a young age, took his mind horribly early. The door swings open: a woman wearing a headscarf, her face obscured. I think this is her. I jump up from my seat, my legs weak, open my mouth but then she removes her headscarf and I see my mistake. I sit down again and drum my fingers on the tabletop. My thoughts turn to Alice, wondering where she is, and hoping she's OK whilst a small, selfish part of me, hopes she's far from OK, that she's regretting her anger and her haste, and is missing me. Because, boy, am I missing her. My every fibre aches for her. And that, in truth, is my life at that moment – caught between two women, two women who have walked out on me, twenty years apart. But I refuse to allow myself to be the victim here, I can not afford to become too self-pitying. They both needed to leave, they both had their reasons, and maybe that reason was me. I knew for sure that Mum would be feeling as nervous as me right now. Maybe even more so. Question is, did she have the strength to see this through? I imagine her approaching the café, her heart equally as fragile as mine, and realising she couldn't face seeing me, that it was all too much. She couldn't do that. She had to do this; I couldn't go through this a second time. George approaches me. 'Is this a special lady you're waiting for?' he asks with a wink.

'No, no,' I say quickly. 'Just my mother.'

'Oh?' He's wondering why I look so shot at, I can tell, but he tries his best to cover it up. 'That's nice,' he says brightly. 'Enjoy!'

He turns to leave and bumps into someone, a woman. He apologises and spins off like a top. The woman looks at me. 'Hello, Thomas.'

I jump up again. 'Oh, hi. Hello.' She smiles at me, exposing incredibly white teeth. 'G-glad you could make it. Take a seat.'

'Thank you.' We both sit. She removes her coat. 'Lovely place this. Is it one of your regulars?'

'Yeah, it is.'

She shuffles in her seat, twists a ring around her finger. 'Thanks for agreeing to see me, Thomas. I know this isn't easy – for either of us.'

'You're here now. Would you like a coffee? They do all the different types. And a cake maybe? George's carrot cake is famous in these parts.'

She looks up at the huge blackboard behind the counter. She's exactly as I remember her, as if she hasn't aged in the last two decades. Her hair, faintly red, is longer now, down to her shoulders, her eyebrows finely arched, crow's feet around her eyes, her perfect teeth, and she's tanned after so many years under the Spanish sun. She's got a kind face, a gentle aura about her and I know I'm going to like her. She's wearing less make-up than I remember.

George saunters over, a large grin fixed on his face, and takes our order. We watch him leave, knowing that it's just the two of us now. She talks about the area and how it's changed since she left. But that she saw a couple of shops that were here in her day and still, by the looks of it, going strong. 'I even popped my head around the door of your barbershop, Thomas. Very nice, what a place. You must be very proud of your achievement there.'

I am proud that I have her approval. I tell her about the shop, and how it came about. Then, somehow, I tell her about my past, going back over the years a step at a time, to the point I was nine years old.

'Have you come back?' I ask her, a flutter of nerves batting in my stomach. 'Or is it just a visit?'

'I want to come back, yes. Perhaps not…'

'Yes?' I realise at this moment just how important her answer is to me, how I want her to say that she's staying here and not returning to Spain.

'Well, perhaps not to this area. It holds too many… memories for me. But to England, to London, yes, certainly. I hope so.'

It's a start, I think, the intention is there.

She sips her coffee, eyeing me over the rim of the cup. 'So, how is your father?'

'Yeah, well, it's, erm, a long story.'

She shrugs her shoulders. 'I have the time if you have…'

I take a large gulp of my coffee, fortifying myself. 'OK, if you're sure…' And so I tell her, tell her of his anguish after she left, of how he never truly recovered. I told her about our time together in the house, just him and me, how difficult it was at times. How I lost so many friends because no one ever liked coming round to my house, because it was so miserable. I told her about how we ate the same dinner night after night after night. Dad never thought to buy me anything. If I grew out of my clothes, I had to ask him, beg him, to buy me new or at least a semi-decent second-hand set. And how he made a fuss as if it was *my fault* for growing. I tell her how Dad used to go to the pub. At first, he only went once or twice a week, and never stayed too long. But then, he started going more often and staying out later and later. He never once thought of getting me a babysitter.

I used to hate being in that horrible house all by myself. I'd watch TV until I was too tired to keep my eyes open. But I could never get to sleep all alone in the house. I'd lay in bed waiting for Dad to return from the pub and then, finally, I could let go and fall asleep. So I was never getting enough sleep, given my age, and my teachers always told me off for going to bed too late. Of course, they never said anything to Dad because he never, not once, came to a parents' evening. He took no interest in my schooling. I'd always present him with my school reports and I was never worried that they were always awful because Dad never read one, not a word. Gee, I'd thought a lot about my upbringing after Mum had left over the years but it was only now, relating all in one hit to my mother I realised just how malnourished I was – nutritionally, mentally, physically, academically, and, most of all, emotionally.

'Oh, Thomas, I'm so sorry.'

'But he was ill, Mum. I…' I stop, we both stop, realising this is the first time I've called her that to her face in twenty bloody years: *Mum*. Just saying it sounds weird.

She places her hand over mine. 'What do you mean he was ill?'

'*Is* ill…' And so I relate to her everything about Dad's early dementia, about how it got slowly but progressively worse until I was told by a health professional that for Dad's sake, as well as mine, he needed to be in a home, being cared for by trained carers.

She listens intently, her eyes welling up. After I finish, we sit in silence for what feels like an age, the soft jazz music and hubbub of the café behind us. Eventually, I break the silence. 'So, what happened, Mum? Why did you leave us?'

She sighs heavily. 'You know why I left you, son. I told you.'

'What?'

'Did you never read my letters?'

'Letters?'

And we both know in that same moment what's happened here. 'You never got them, did you?'

I shake my head. We sit in silence for a while. George is

busy serving a table of three girls behind me, they giggle as he flirts with them with his campness on full display. He is funny. But right now, there's a very large hole in my heart with the realisation of what happened – my father hid my mother's letters from me. The more I think of this, the more something bubbles up inside of me. How dare he? Did he think he was protecting me? He had no right, however young I was, I was entitled to read my mother's letters to me.

'How often did you write?'

'Two or three times a year.'

I allow myself time to absorb this. 'So, why did you leave, Mum?'

Mum stares out of the window watching a man push his bicycle up the street. She takes a deep breath and exhales. Then, when she turns back to face me, she is crying. 'Your father was a violent man, Thomas.'

Her words hit me like a fist. 'Dad?'

She nods. 'Yes.'

I can't process this. 'He hit you?'

She nods again. I believe her. I still find it hard to process but I don't doubt her for a second; I know she's telling the truth. My accident-prone mother, always falling over, always bumping into things, always tripping over. My mother who always wore so much make-up. Of course, it all makes sense now. She wasn't accident-prone at all, and she had no choice than to cake herself in make-up. My bastard father. I want to stand up, to pace around. I want to shout, scream this place down.

Mum plays with a paper tube of sugar. 'I knew I had to leave. But… I once made the mistake of threatening to take you with me. He said he'd kill me, Thomas. Your father said he'd track me down and kill me. And, you know, I believed him. I knew I'd never be able to protect you, not properly, and we'd forever be on the run, looking over our shoulders. I knew I was leaving you behind with a violent man but I knew he never hit you. I just had to pray that he never would.'

'No, he never hit me.'

'I had to choose. I had to decide what was the safest option, to leave you with this man or take you with me into an uncertain future. I called social services once but nothing came of it. I had very little money, he made sure of that, and no idea of where to go. But I did it, Thomas. I had to go. Kissing you goodnight that night was *the* hardest thing I've ever had to do. Please...' She reaches for my hand again. 'Please, Thomas, forgive me...'

'You ended up in Spain? Did you remarry, have another family?'

'No. There was a man for a while but... it never worked out. We didn't work hard enough for what we wanted, we just allowed it to slip through our fingers. I still regret it.'

Why do those words seem so apt to me right at this moment?

'But,' says Mum. 'Nothing on earth compares to the regret I felt on leaving you, Thomas. Nothing...'

Chapter 18: Mac

I storm into the care home, bumping into Patsy, the carer. 'Hi, Mr…' She doesn't have chance to finish the sentence. Passing through the dining room, I see Alice's grandmother. She recognises me and waves. I take no notice of her or anyone. I have narrow vision like a horse with blinkers. I charge into the conservatory but Dad isn't here, the chair he usually sits on is empty. I ask one of the other patients, the younger man in the wheelchair, but he just shrugs and returns his attention to the lunchtime news blaring out on the mounted TV.

I go upstairs and head for Dad's bedroom, even though, as a visitor, I'm not allowed to. I charge into Dad's room without knocking but the room is empty. It's a tiny room, barely room for the bed and a wardrobe. There's nothing in this room to show who sleeps in here – no photographs, no knick knacks or mementos, no books or magazines or anything. I hadn't really thought about it before but I'm seeing Dad in a new light now, and this room shows a man without history, a head devoid of memories and a heart devoid of love. It is, like him, an empty shell. It should instil a sense of sadness or *something* but it does not, it merely enrages me further.

I trot back downstairs, my ears on full alert, listening out for his voice. I stomp back into the conservatory and this time… he's there, sitting in his chair looking out over the garden wearing his dark red cardigan and his corduroy trousers. My blood boils on seeing him there. Butter wouldn't melt. It's a horrific moment when you realise the villain in your life was the good guy after all, and the saviour in your life turns out to have been the monster, the cause of all your misery. It explains so much, why Mum wore so much make-up, she was hiding the bruises caused by this bastard. Did he hate all women? Is that why he was so foul when I introduced him to Alice? He'd not only chased Mum away, but he'd also chased Alice away. God knows where she was. And still, he sits here, waiting for his robin, without a care in the world, totally unaware of the chaos he causes, the trail of destruction he leaves in his wake. Well, no more, Dad, it ends here.

'Hello, Dad,' I say in a booming voice.

I stand in front of him, hands on hips, looking down at him, wanting to intimidate him with my height. He does look weaker, paler. He looks as if he's lost a lot of weight, he looks ill, but I don't care, I really don't care. He looks up and recognises me but says nothing. He knows something's changed here.

'I want you to know this is my last visit.'

'Hey?'

'I know, Dad, I know everything. I know you were a violent, wife-beating bastard.'

'Fuck off!' he shouts. 'Go on, get out of here. Fuck off.'

'You hit my mother.'

I can see in my peripheral vision someone coming to see what's happening.

'She was weak, always so weak. She fuckin' deserved whatever was coming to her. Still does, the bitch.'

My fists clench. I want to hit him; I want to kill him. 'You bastard.'

'Mr McIntosh,' shouts Mrs Hale, the manager. Is she referring to me or Dad? 'What's all this shouting and swearing?' Patsy is behind her.

I don't look at them, my eyes boring into Dads'. He holds my gaze only for a second or two before turning away.

'What's happening here, Mr McIntosh?' Mrs Hale asks me, her tone sharp. Patsy hovers nervously behind her.

'Nothing,' I say, like a truculent school child, my attention still fixed on the man I used to call Dad.

'I can't have my clients being upset. Patsy here heard your father swearing. What have you said to your father? You know how poorly he is. Your poor father.'

'Father? This piece of shit is no father to me.'

'Mr McIntosh!' The shock is evident in her voice. 'I can't allow language like that in here. I'm sorry but any more and I'll have to ask you to leave.'

'I'm going, don't you worry.' I look back at my father for the last time, not realising until this very moment that I was so capable of hate. 'She deserved someone so much better than you. Goodbye, Dad.'

Some recognition hits him, as if his brain is processing what's happening, that his only relative, his only visitor and contact with the outside world is leaving. 'No, wait, son, please not like this. Wait, please. Please…'

But I don't wait. Ignoring his pleas, I leave.

I step outside and breathe in the chilly north London air. I feel great. I want to punch the air. Instead, I quietly say to myself, 'That was for you, Mum.'

I return to my shop. My head is pounding. I don't know what to do with myself. I need a break, a few days away from London, a change of scene. I'm going to go back to my flat and lie on the sofa scrolling through my phone until I find somewhere remote I can escape to for a couple of days, somewhere rural, in the middle of nowhere. First, I need to check in with Eoin and Tony.

I find them both busy with customers. They greet me cautiously. I check everything's OK but I need never worry with these two around. 'Listen, guys, I need to go away for a few days. I've got to get my head sorted.'

They both nod. They understand.

'I'm sorry. I know it puts the two of you under more pressure. I should have found someone by now. I've just got distracted by things recently.'

'We'll manage,' says Eoin.

'It's OK, Mac, don't worry,' says Tony, fishing his vape from his pocket.

They're good lads, both of them. I smile. 'Right then…'

Eoin says, 'Before you go though, Mac, there's someone who needs to speak to you in the office.'

'There is?'

They exchange knowing glances. 'Go see.'

I step into the office with some trepidation. He stands on seeing me. 'Hi, Mac.'

'Jack. You all right? What brings you here?'

'Two things, Mac. Two important things.'

'Christ, that sounds ominous. Shall we sit?' We both do. 'So, go on. Shoot.'

He clasps his massive hands together. 'I could see how

worried you were earlier about Alice, so er… I rang her.'

My heart speeds up a notch. 'You did? What did she say?'

'I asked her if everything was all right and where she was. She said what she said earlier, about needing to get away for a while, about stuff getting on top of her. She said she was staying at her parents' place in a place called Keswick in the–'

'Lake District. Her parents own a hairdresser there.'

'Yeah, that was it, the Lake District. Listen, it's not for me to tell you what to do, Mac, but I reckon you need to get your arse up to Keswick as soon as. Get a train from Euston, they go often enough.'

'I'm going now, mate.'

'I told her Ian's furious with her but she didn't care, said something she didn't expect to have to deal with sexual harassment in the workplace in this day and age. In other words, Mac, she's jacked her job in.'

'Hell.'

'She's not the only one,' he says quietly.

'What?'

'I've jacked in my job too.'

'You what?'

'The man had fairly well fired me anyway because I told him to keep his grubby hands off of Alice. So, basically, he told me to fuck off. I said, no problem, I didn't want to work for a twat like him anyway.'

I laugh.

'So, er, I was wondering, Mac, if you er…'

'You want your old job back?' I shout. 'Is that it? After you walked out on me, you come in here and say you want your job back?'

He turns red, not liking the tone of my voice. I stand up and open my arms. 'Come here, you great oaf.'

He didn't expect that. His eyes turn red as he stumbles to his feet. We hug, a great big bear hug between two great big men. 'Of course you can have your job back, mate. I couldn't be happier.'

'Thanks, Mac. I'm sorry… you know.'

'It's fine. Really.'

We part, both slightly embarrassed, I think.

'You ought to go, Mac, catch that train.'

'I know.' I pat my pockets, making sure I had everything I needed before heading home to pack a small suitcase. 'You want to start again tomorrow?'

'I'll start now if you want?'

'Yeah! Yeah, that'd be great, mate. Eoin and Tony will be so happy!' I slap him on the arm. 'Welcome home, Jack. It's good to have you back.'

Chapter 19: Mac

It took three and a half hours on the train from Euston to Keswick. I sat by myself, watching the world rush by, listening to music on my earphones, rehearsing what I wanted to say to Alice. I spoke to Mum by phone as we drew out of Euston. It felt good to hear her voice again. She told me she was spending the day flat hunting. More importantly, she said she was feeling better about life than she'd done in many, many years. And that, she said, was down to me. I told her she'd had a similar effect on me. I didn't tell her that I almost beat the shit out of the man who had made her life such a misery, and I didn't tell her that I was determined not to have two women walk out on me. One had come back, for which I was very happy, now it was down to me to find the other and bring her home.

The train draws into Keswick. It's late afternoon, and I know I need to hurry if I'm to find the hairdressers before it closes for the day.

I jump off the train and walk briskly through the tiny ticket hall and out into the village. The first thing I notice is the air, how fresh it smells. I breathe it down into my lungs and feel its goodness. The evening sun bathes Keswick in a gentle, amber light. It must be market day – stalls either side of a pedestrian street, lots of people strolling, while the stallholders start packing up for the day. I walk the length of the main street, looking at the shops behind the stalls, looking for a hairdresser. I see a lovely old building at the end of the street which, according to a large sign above the main doors, is called the Moot Hall. It looks like a church and has a tower. It has a clock on the tower which, oddly enough, only has one hand. Did the other drop off? Weird. Anyway, I'm not here to be a tourist; I have a job to do, and that job is to save my life from being barren and lonely for ever more.

I see a hairdresser, imaginatively called Keswick Hair. I step inside. It's busy, despite the lateness of the day, all women, staff and customers, and they turn their heads when they hear my voice. I'm a big bloke with a big voice and a big beard, women do tend to stare at me, sometimes, yes, out of lust, but more often, I think, out of curiosity. It's fine either way, I really don't mind. So, I ask the young girl on reception for Alice, the daughter of a woman who owns a hairdresser in Keswick. She shakes her head, not here, have I tried Barbarella's down the road. I hadn't. I thank her and with a nod at the ladies under the driers, I make my exit.

Barbarella's is fairly close by. I step inside. It has a nice, modern feel to it: shiny wooden floor, huge gilt-edged mirrors, everything glossy and clean. Again, several women turn and look at me. 'We're about to close,' says the woman behind the reception desk without looking up. She's an older woman, perhaps in her fifties. She looks up at me. 'Oh, I say,' she says in a totally different tone.

'Hi.'

'Well, hello. How can I help you?'

'I'm looking for a… a friend.'

'I see…'

'I believe her parents own a hairdresser in this town. Her name is Alice.'

'Alice, you say?' She knows Alice, it's obvious.

'Yes. She lives in Holloway in London but–'

'She's my daughter. Alice Sinclair.'

'Oh? Right.' I'm not sure what to say next, in case Alice has told her about me, and painted me in a bad light.

'Is your name Mac by any chance?'

I feel as if I'm turning red under this woman's scrutiny. 'Yes, that's me.'

She smiles. 'She's talked about nothing but you.'

'Really? Nice things or…?'

'Oh yes, indeed. You've made quite an impression on my daughter.' She looks me up and down. 'I can see why.'

I smile. 'Is there any chance of speaking to your daughter, Mrs Sinclair?'

She giggles. 'Oh, call me Liz, please. And of course you can speak to her; she'll be delighted.'

'I'm not so sure.'

'Let me give her a shout.'

She trots off. I stand there, rocking on the balls of my feet, and vaguely smile at the women having their hair done. I hear Liz calling for her daughter, telling her she had a visitor but not saying my name. I hear Alice's echoey voice calling back in response and just the sound of her voice makes me go weak at the knees. I hear her footsteps on a set of stairs and a heat rises through me. 'Who is it?' she asks.

Her mother doesn't answer, just sweeps her hand towards where I'm standing.

Alice stops in her tracks and lets out a strange sort of yelp on seeing me. Her hand reaches for her heart. 'Oh, my, Mac, oh.'

Alice's mother and every other woman in the shop is listening to this now, their heads turning from Alice to me as they await my response.

'Hi, Alice.' I want to charge across this wooden floor and collect her in my arms and lift her high. But I can't, not yet, not until I am sure of where I stand. 'I hope you don't mind me calling on you like this.'

Her eyes are like saucers, such is her shock on seeing me. 'No, no, it's... It's a surprise, I have to say, I mean, I didn't expect... What are you doing here?'

'Well, that first time I met you, you did say Keswick is a beautiful place and that I ought to visit it sometime So... here I am.'

'Yes, here you are.'

'Could we go out for a coffee or something?'

'Erm...' She glances over at her mother who shrugs in return. 'Sure. I'll just get my...' She's about to go back to fetch her coat when she stops. 'Actually, no. I don't want a coffee right now.'

'Tea then?'

'No, nothing. I want to... Why don't you come upstairs to my room?' She looks at all the women watching our little drama playing out. 'We'll have more privacy up there. Come...'

I don't need a second invitation. Alice's mother smiles nervously as I pass her. I step into a cavernous space from which there's a staircase. Alice is already at the top, out of view. I follow her up two flights. She's waiting for me at a bedroom door on the second floor. She doesn't speak but slips into the room. I enter.

It's her bedroom OK, her childhood bedroom with a single bed under the window. There're posters of pop bands now defunct and largely forgotten, thick purple carpet, lots of fluffy cushions on the bed, garish and girly colours, but warm and inviting. And now I am here, standing in her room, opposite Alice, not sure what I'm expecting to happen. We stare at each other, no words, and a surge of electricity passes between us. Then something snaps and we are in each other's arms, kissing.

Chapter 20: Alice

Mac pushes me backwards until I'm pressed against the wall next to the window. His lips are on mine, we kiss greedily, desperately, as if our lives depend on it. My arms pull him closer and my fingernails dig into his back through his shirt. I can feel his erection as it presses into me. I can't wait to free it, to see his meat in front of me, in my hand. I arch my head up and he kisses my neck. He cups my breasts and forces his face between them. I start to unbutton my shirt, fumbling with excitement. Mac gives me a hand, and eventually, between us, we've managed it. He admires my lilac-coloured bra but only for a second or two before I whip it off, flinging it to one side. My nipples, pink and hard, are waiting to be sucked. He doesn't disappoint, cupping a breast and clamping his mouth over the nipple, suckling hard, whilst tweaking the other between his fingers. Oh hell, that goes right to my pussy.

I pull down his zipper. He hastily kicks off his shoes before unbuckling his belt and pulling down his jeans. The front of his boxers are wet with precum. I pull them down and watch with utter fascination and excitement as his dick is freed. Oh wow, his cock is rock hard now, the veins pulsing. I kneel down and gently lick the droplets of precum from the tip of his cock. Fuck, he's big. I'm going to have to be extremely wet to accommodate the full length here. My heart is racing just at the thought of it.

He removes his shirt, exposing his firm, muscular chest, his abs ripple as he moves. I'm so wet for him, I've never experienced this intensity of lust and longing before. I know I will do anything this man asks of me, not just now, today, but for ever more.

'I'm sorry, Mac,' I whisper. 'I shouldn't have taken it out on you.'

'No, you were right. It just took me a long time to realise my father's not… not a good man. *I'm* sorry. I don't care who it is, no one, and I mean *no one*, speaks to you like that.'

'I want you so bad,' I say.

'Yes, the same, I feel the same.'

We step over to the bed. In quick fluid motions, I remove the rest of my clothes. Naked now, we lie on the bed, him on top, kissing me hard, his left hand kneading my breast. He inches down my body, planting kisses on my nipples, on my stomach and down, deliciously down. My body tingles under his magical touch. He gasps on seeing my glistening cunt and he knows that I'm desperate to be touched. I raise my hips, inviting him in. Gently, he presses his lips into me, his tongue sliding up and down my swollen clit. I groan loudly. I could die in this moment. My hips gyrate and my groaning amplifies and I'm on the cusp of coming. Slowly, he inserts a finger inside me while sucking on my labia. I gasp and grunt as he moves up to my clitoris. I grind myself further onto him, suffocating him in the warm, wet heaven that is my pussy. I writhe and groan and call out his name over and over. My fingers clasp the back of his head pushing him even harder into the gorgeous wetness of my snatch.

Then, I pull away, lean up and reach for my bedside drawers. Quickly, I remove a condom from its wrapper and pass it to Mac. He pulls it down and over his solid dick. He edges his cock closer to my entrance. 'Are you ready?' he says.

'Fuck, have I ever been so ready?'

Inch by inch he enters me. I yelp, my back arched up. The walls of my pussy squeezes his shaft. He whispers my name as he pushes his entire length into me. Oh, shit!

'Are you OK, Alice?'

'Yes, yes, fuck yes.'

'I'll take it gently.'

'Don't you fucking dare.'

Boy, I asked for it! He pumps and he pumps hard, and each time I cry out. Our rhythm quickly escalates. I widen my legs, and again, as wide as I can, giving him full access to that wet cunt of mine. I judder beneath him. 'Mac, I'm coming,' I gasp, pulling on his hair. 'I'm coming.'

'So am I.' I can feel his intensity and urgency as the cum rises up his shaft and I want to hold off until he comes first but I have no control over it.

'I'm coming. Oh my God, Mac. Kiss me, kiss me.'

He plants his lips on mine as my body shakes beneath him. I silently scream into him, our kiss muffling the scream. Seconds later, he explodes. He pounds his semen into me, pump after pump after pump. I can feel him relax on top of me as he shoots his last drops into me. We've done it. My God, that was just fantastic. I feel well and truly fucked. Mac remains within me for a minute or two, kissing my cheek, making sure I'm all right. We laugh as we catch our breaths, exhausted but happy. Very happy. I cannot remember a time when I felt happier than this, and it's all down to this wonderful, handsome, caring man, Mac, my lovely Mac.

Epilogue
Two weeks later

Bertie's Café is heaving with customers with all the work-types coming in for their lunch. Alice and I wait, holding hands, our eyes flicking from each other to the café door. More customers come in wanting takeouts. The noise is loud, everyone talking at the same time.

'How are you feeling, darling?' asks Alice.

'Fine, just fine.' She squeezes my hand under the table. I've waited a long time for this moment. We're both a little nervous even though I know I have no reason to be.

'Look at you two,' says George, bringing us our coffees. 'Love's young dream.'

A short while later, I see her. I stand as she approaches and we smile at each other and I know this is going to go well.

'Thomas!' She stands on tiptoe and gives me a kiss.

'Mum, this beautiful woman here is Alice.'

Alice stands and the two don't hesitate – they hug, and for a moment I think I might shed a tear.

We all sit, and George, smiling like a Cheshire cat, brings

another coffee.

We talk about lots of different things. Mum's moved into a lovely flat not too far away, and she's going on a date tonight, and is feeling excited and apprehensive about it at the same time. Alice too is about to embark on a new venture – a new job, not as a hairdresser, but working in PR for some swanky West End marketing firm. They will work her hard but they'll pay her handsomely and she's happy. I tell Mum that Jack is back working for me. She's not met Jack but that doesn't stop me from telling her about the four of us, Jack, Tony, Eoin and me, the Four Musketeers, reunited and doing great!

'And, Thomas,' my mother says to me in an earnest tone and I know what's coming. She puts her hand over mine. 'Are you OK?'

'Yeah.'

'How was it? How did it go?'

'I almost didn't go. I didn't feel the need to. But I did – if only to make sure it was true, that he really was dead and could do no one any more harm. It was just me, and Mrs Hale and Patsy from the care home. No one else. No other family, no partner, no friends, no one but us. And, you know, I know he'd been a bastard to you, Mum, and he didn't deserve any sympathy, but watching his coffin disappear behind those curtains, I felt this wave of sadness for him. For so long he was all I had at home. I didn't know then that he was so bad and that he'd beaten you up and hid all your letters to me, he was just Dad. Dad and me against the world. I know he suffered himself when he was a kid. He told me occasionally that his father had a temper on him, and I just felt sorry for him for a moment.' I took a large gulp of coffee.

Mum pats my hand. 'Thank you for going, Mac. I know it couldn't have been easy for you.'

'No, but, you know, everything's easier nowadays…'

We both turn and smile at Alice.

'You have something else to tell your mother, Mac,' says Alice.

'Yes.'

Mum looks from Alice to me. 'Oh yes? And what's that?'

I take Alice's hand and kiss it. She smiles at me. 'We're getting married.'

'Oh, Thomas, Alice, oh, what wonderful news…'

George, passing by, balancing a tray on his fingertips, hears this. 'Huh? Did I hear properly? Oh, I'm sorry, this is *your* moment. I am such a buffoon.' He bows.

Alice laughs. 'Don't be silly, it's fine.'

'You're the second person to know now, George,' I say.

He beams with pride. 'I say everyone should know this happy news.'

'What do you mean?'

He puts the tray down and claps loudly. The whole café goes quiet. 'Hold up, everyone, hold up. Please, Mac and Lady Mac, do stand a moment.' Alice and I, giggling, do as we're told.

'Ladies and gentleman,' says George in a booming voice. 'A moment of your time please. Raise your cups or your glasses or your false teeth, whatever it is, because these two beautiful people here… are getting married!'

The whole café erupts in cheers. My mother wipes her eyes. Alice hugs me. I raise my own mug at everyone as they clap and shout our names. I look into Alice's eyes and I know I love her, and I know I always will.

The End

The Barbershop Quartet

The First Cut
The Next Cut
The Deepest Cut
The Final Cut

ARRyder.com

To obtain Ashley's short story / prequel to The Barbershop Quartet, *The Original Cut*, and join his Mailing List and be the first to know of future releases, etc, please go to:

https://www.arryder.com/free-book